Reviews

"[Hahn's] choices create a satisfying sensory experience as the protagonist seeks a real and present version of himself. An engrossing, hallucinatory relationship story."

— *STARRED Kirkus Reviews*

"Moving between hypnotic episodes of unreality and riveting scenes of stark daily life, this is a gripping and remarkable story, both gritty and graceful."

— Eugenia Kim, author of *The Kinship of Secrets*

"Eddie is one of those characters, like Holden Caulfield in *Catcher in the Rye,* or Celie in *The Color Purple,* whom you want to hug and tell everything is going to be all right, even though you know he has to find that out for himself. Because you love Eddie from the first page, you will read on, guided by Hahn's sure hand, in this remarkable debut novel."

— Pete Nelson, author of *I Thought You Were Dead*

"T.E. Hahn delivers Eddie's story with sharp wit and incisive humor, as well as incredible heart and emotional richness. His writing is sparse and lyrical, emphasizing the importance of every word, and his ability to paint vivid, disquieting images will leave the reader with much to reflect on long after the final page. Eddie's journey is one well worth coming along for."

— Stephanie Harper, editor/author of *Sermon Series*

"T.E. Hahn's remarkable debut novel is one of those rare books that will attract both YA and adult readers. The novel's dark atmospheric effects, staccato but often poetic prose, and challenging narrative devices clearly mark this ambitious book as one of emotional and psychological heft. Eddie's story reflects our own PTSD age.

— Michael C. White, author of *Soul Catcher* and *Resting Places*

"*Open My Eyes* is a swift fever dream of a novel...Readers will root for Eddie to defy all that binds him and define his own reality, his own truth about what love means."

— Rachel Basch, author of *The Listener*

OPEN MY EYES

By T.E. Hahn

Open My Eyes text copyright © T.E. Hahn
Edited by Andrew DiPrinzio

Published in North America and Europe by Running Wild Press. Visit Running Wild Press at www.runningwildpress.com Educators, librarians, book clubs (as well as the eternally curious), go to www.runningwildpress.com for teaching tools.

ISBN (pbk) 978-1-947041-28-8
ISBN (ebook) 978-1-947041-43-1

Printed in the United States of America.

1.

In the beginning was Elizabeth, and Elizabeth was in light, and Elizabeth was light.

She sat between the conductor and trumpets in the band room. Her brown hair glowed with her freckles, her eyes level with my chest. Short, unpainted fingernails searched for the cold brass keys on the saxophone while her lips tightly pursed around her mouthpiece. My medicated gaze and mohawk usually frightened girls, but not her.

Besides Elizabeth, what I loved most about high school was playing the drums, being able to control, push, drag, and stop time. In the pocket of a song, I was a wave leading a wall of sound to shore. The musical director noticed my love and asked me to help the 9th and 10th grade jazz band drummers after school.

That was when I first saw her.

She was in the instrument storage room after rehearsal when I approached her for the first time.

"My mom would kill me," were the first words she said to me. "You're a junior."

"It's only a two year difference," I said. "You think your mom will have a problem with my mohawk?"

She smiled. "Yes, but not as much as your age."

"I'll shave it off today," I said. "I'll shave off years of my life for you."

Elizabeth tugged on her earlobe, which was slightly bigger than the other. "It's ok. It only matters what I think."

"And what do you think?" I said.

She placed her sax in its case and gazed up at me. The lights in the room melted around her like butter on warm popcorn. I swam between her freckles.

"I think you're funny."

She crackled in my chest like carbonation all evening. And so, unable to sleep that night, I took my evening dose of medication and hurried out of the house after Mom had fallen asleep.

Bird songs echoed from the darkness like bursts of light from a lack of oxygen as I walked the blacktop to her house. At the end of my street, someone had spray painted 'Wake up, you'll find what you're looking for' on the pavement. It was old and faded, but still legible. I continued walking, hoping I would find Elizabeth's house before it rained. After band rehearsal, she had mentioned she lived on Mimicry Lane, no more than a few miles from my house, but I didn't know, or couldn't remember, her house number, and the homes on her block were dark in the night. Even white houses looked gray. The moon was hidden, the only light a lone streetlamp that stood at the end of the lane. It was a short street, seven houses connecting two parallel side streets. I unzipped my jacket, warm from the walk, took my woolen gloves off, stuffed them in my pocket, and wandered down the street looking through windows. I prayed Elizabeth might be outside admiring the stars so I could admire her as my own burning light in the dark. She seemed the type who liked constellations and comets.

I hid behind a short, wide bush outside a home with a brightly lit living room. A gray-haired couple sat in front of a television set. The old woman trimmed the old man's silvery back. Clumps of hair gathered on the buzzer and fell, gathered and fell, gathered and fell. I carried on down the street, picturing Elizabeth thirty years from now, shaving my back, her earlobe glowing silver in the moonlight entering through the window, her warm freckles—

Then I saw her.

The third house on the block. A light blue ranch. A colorful, life-like miniature gnome stood at the base of her steps with a knowing smile. A large maple tree reached across her front lawn. Its roots had broken through the cement sidewalk. I hid behind it and watched from just across her narrow front lawn. The living room was a long rectangle, the walls the color of dirty snow. Her mother sat on the couch watching television—a short, stocky woman with shoulder-length blond hair in a Star-Trek bathrobe. The ceiling lights glossed the hair on her upper lip. Elizabeth's father was in the background, in the kitchen, cooking with his bald, slippery head engulfed in a billow of steam.

And then there was Elizabeth—standing, glowing, lighting some of the darkness just outside the living room window. She was light. She stood to the left of her mother, looking up at the ceiling as if waiting for it to rain. And then it did. A drop fell from the ceiling, rolled down her forehead, down her cheek. A few more gave way to a steady trickle on her. She stepped aside. Her mom stood and yelled. Fragments of her muffled shouts reached me: "Idiot—move away—get in here." Her mother closed the Captain Spock section of robe across her body. Her father turned his moist head from the steam and rushed into the living room. There they were, all three, silent, standing in the middle of the room, staring up at the ceiling, watching the water drip from a cracked sky.

Headlights illuminated my body. A car honked as it drove alongside me. I fell over a surfaced root. The shadow driver lowered the passenger-side window.

"Fuckin' Creeper!"

I looked back into Elizabeth's living room. The three of them came to the window and peered like possums drawn to darkness, their eyes wide, black and glassy.

Elizabeth opened a window and called, "Is that you?"

Was "you" me? How did she know? I was still and heard the "you" echo with the bird nocturnes—*you, you, you*—is that you who will save me? Is that you who will love me? Is that you who will come to fix the sky, and make it stop raining, or make it flood?

Shame on me, but I just ran, and ran, and ran, and kept running, even after I got home that night, through tosses and turns, through the sound of Mom's snores, through sleep, and medicated dreams, and Elizabeth staring up at a cracked sky—waiting.

Falling rain fell to falling snow. I'd just received my driver's license, and I'd promised Elizabeth that I would attend her winter band concert. We stood in the center of the high school's cafeteria waiting for her moment to play when the red-faced band director barged through the double-wide doors. "Everyone in band, get on stage."

Elizabeth reached out her hand, barely grazed the hairs on my wrist, then retreated quickly as if startled by my realness. "How are you, Eddie?"

"When I'm looking at you, I feel like that band director is sitting on my chest."

She laughed, but had to go. We hadn't reached the kissing stage. I wanted to say something to her, something epic, wanted to tell her I loved her, though I hardly knew her, wanted to kiss her before she left. I was never good at timing. All I could say was, "Your dress is pretty." I knew it wasn't a dress, but I said it anyway.

"It's not a dress, silly. It's new. Here, feel it. It's soft."

She grabbed my fingertips with her hand and she rubbed them up and down her velour arm. I trembled—goose bumps.

"Does this mean we're 'together'?" I asked.

She giggled and scrunched her nose. Then she vanished as fast as shadow in fog.

I sat at a cafeteria table feeling lightheaded. It was late. Twenty or so students across the room waited for their moment, their conversations a soft buzz mixed with the distant hum of muffled drums in my head like a dizzy spell. The muted brassy horns of the band echoed from the stage.

Your Mom was written in newly inked black marker on the table in front of me. I put my head down, feeling faint.

I opened my eyes in a deli booth with a sore forehead, freezing, feeling like I had been kicked in the stomach. The door to the deli was partially held open by the wind, which soared through it and laid goose eggs on my neck and forearms. I often found myself sitting by open doors, thresholds with freezing wind or rain or snow pouring through them, but always an open door, waiting for someone to walk through.

The store was filled with empty tables. On the other side of the frost-lined window were five copper-skinned men with greasy hair and ripped woolen hats. They huddled close to the window of a pickup truck. A pale man in the passenger's seat was talking to them, writing something down on paper with a yellow smile and a bead of sweat clinging to his brow. The five shivering, copper-skinned men were huddled in formation as if waiting for a quarterback to give them a play. A drop of tea sat in a Styrofoam cup in front of me next to a shopping list written in my handwriting:

~~—those things that hold together wires and things…what the hell is the name? Little ropes. I'll come back to it…~~

-*Chicken breast boneless*
-*V-day card*
-*low sugar ketchup*
twist ties—little ropes are twist ties

"Yo, buddy," a voice said.

A large man in a tangerine colored vest with hands like sledgehammers stared at me.

"Yes?"

"Your mom is on your forehead." He stared at the top of my head with a smile like Elizabeth's lawn gnome. Then he laughed as he headed outside into the cold toward the truck.

I licked my palm and felt for my forehead. I rubbed hard and turned my hand. It was smeared black—School. Elizabeth. The concert. Days ago? Years ago? I could still feel her hand holding my fingers against the soft velour of her outfit. Then my cold fingers tingled. I opened and closed my fist to revive my hand.

A deli worker behind the counter changed the channel on the T.V. A commercial for a car dealership advertised a sale: "Like young love, this deal won't last." The local news appeared. A pale woman stood next to a lake reporting on a father who had drowned trying to save his son. He had broken through the lake's ice and drowned as well. "A tragedy on this holiday," she added.

At the bottom right of the screen: *February 14, 9:35 am.* The chilling wind from the open door blanketed my body again.

Outside the deli, the copper men spoke to the construction workers in the truck. Their breath formed specters. I searched for a pen in my breast pocket, but found something else, something bulky. A roll of bright orange twine. A Déjà vu. I put it back in my pocket, sucked the last cold drop out of the cup, and left the deli back out into the cold.

2.

Before the beginning, you died, and medication was prescribed, and medication was life.

I might have known who you were at some point. I can't remember much. Mom has only revealed pieces of you like a shattered stained glass church window. What was Mom like before you died, Dad? I can't remember that either. Maybe I was too young, or maybe she was too normal. Maybe some things are better left as fragments.

I wonder if you knew you died after you died. I wonder whether you ate ketchup with almost everything, like I do. I never refrigerate it, even though the bottle says to. I don't need to. My apartment is cold enough. I'm freezing. I'm starving. How sickly I've become. I can almost see through myself, like a sliver of white fish in sunlight.

The last morning you were alive appears like headlights hitting reflectors in the night. I sat on our warm kitchen table while you packed your lunch in a brown paper bag. Your dark brown hair was splayed across your forehead. Mom watched you with her hand to her mouth, biting her nails in the entrance of the kitchen.

"Adam, you forgot to shave. Don't get in trouble again," Mom said.

"Better do as Mom says, right Eddo?" you said to me.

You left the room rubbing your chin. Mom came to the kitchen table. I could never tell when she was smiling because of the stroke she'd had in her twenties that left her mouth droopy on one side, like it had been shot with Novocain. Did it bother you never knowing if she was happy?

The sun came through the kitchen window behind me. It cast Mom's face in a dull orange hue. She stroked my cheek. I closed my eyes and wrapped my arms around her. Wind chimes swept through the open window.

"You're going to make a great husband one day," she said.

"Your face is orange," I said, opening my eyes.

"You're going to make some girl very happy."

"I don't like girls."

"You like me, right?"

"Yes," I said.

"And I'm a girl."

"Yes."

"So then you like girls, silly."

"No, I love you, Mom."

The wind rushed through the window and brushed her hair off her forehead. Her eyes shone like amber gems.

"How do I look? Clean and spiffy?" you said from the doorway.

Mom took her hand off my face and turned to you. "You look good," she said.

"How do I look, Eddo?"

You picked me up off the table and sat me in one of the kitchen chairs. A piece of tissue clung to your neck under your chin. A small line of blood drizzled from the cut down your neck. I gave you two thumbs up, and you hugged me.

"Be good for Mommy." You moved close to Mom in the entrance. The orange glow of the rising sun soaked you both. Glimmering specks of dust hovered around your bodies like lightning bugs at dusk. A breeze blew into the window again, made the hairs on the back of my neck stand and hardened my skin, but the wind chimes were gone.

"I love you, Brenda," you said to her.

"Why?" She backed against the frame of the kitchen's entrance.

"You know why," you said. "Do you love me?"

She raised her head. Was she smiling? I know you were. You moved closer, tried to kiss her, but Mom turned her head, and your thin lips met her orange cheek. But Mom was strange like that, and you knew her best.

This was the last time I saw you. A warm Saturday in 1986. Showered in light. An ethereal orange glow—blessed. I couldn't have picked a better memory. Or maybe I have.

For the rest of the day, I played with Matchbox cars on the living room floor, waiting for you to come home. There was a knock at the door. I crawled to the top of the stairs and looked through the banister. Two policemen, one old and one young, stood in front of Mom with moist faces. They spoke so softly that I couldn't hear their words. The younger policeman removed his hat, exposing a mat of brown hair pressed to his scalp with clear gray eyes, like you, Dad—but it wasn't you. He turned the hat in his hands like the wheel of a car without power steering. They glanced at me, and then the older policeman removed his hat. Mom looked up at me too, the animate part of her mouth quivered. She didn't faint, she didn't cry, she didn't close her eyes. The corner of her mouth just twitched as if trying to smile, but the details of a happy memory were receding before her.

"Dad's dead, Eddie."

"What?" I asked.

The older policeman opened his mouth, as if to explain.

"Get out of my house." Mom pushed the men out of the house and slammed the door. Then I heard her bedroom door slam shut.

Slam Shut Slam Shut—this was my childhood.

That was it. That was all she said. No explanation. We just kept living through the cold, the early coming of winter. Should I have kissed you goodbye, said I love you? Hugged you longer? But what I wanted more than anything was to remind you of the bloody tissue still clinging to your neck, just in case you'd forgotten.

A dark chasm opened in the earth. Colorful roses littered the ground.

A large box was lowered into darkness. Mom pulled at her eyebrows, standing in front of the hole. A wasp flew from a flower to an aunt I'd never met. It hovered around her large, black sunhat. The wasp hummed a hymn from far away. She waved at it, then it stung her in the neck and she cried with the wind over the priest's speech about St. Michael and ashes.

Mom took down all of the pictures with you the day after the funeral. That night, after I had pretended to fall asleep, I followed her into the backyard in my pajamas and hid behind a rose bush. Mom wore a jacket over her nightgown with no shoes, her feet browned in earth. She dug a hole in the ground with a small garden shovel and dropped the pictures in, as if your first burial wasn't enough. Through my suspended breath, she struck a match and lit the memories ablaze, whispered something, her eyes wet in the firelight. I didn't say anything. I couldn't. I prayed she'd forgotten a photo.

For some weeks after this, my body sobbed without me knowing it was sobbing. This wasn't grieving, Dad. I knew I missed you, but I didn't understand why. My body knew it had to cry, but grieving is in the knowing. Grieving is something only adults can do. Something I never did. Something Mom and Grandma cheated me out of.

Yearning to grieve is tragic.

3.

Mom's mom, Grandma, though there was nothing grand about her, visited our house one Sunday after we had attended church. I stole a sniff of Mom's drink when she left it in the kitchen. It stung my nose. I never knew she drank the stinging drink. In the living room, they spoke as quietly as they would in church.

"I don't know what to say to him." Mom rocked with her hands to her face.

"Don't say anything. Just don't coddle the boy. He doesn't need that, Brenda," Grandma said.

When I cried those first few months, Mom would pull at her hair and ignore me. I thought that it was my fault. Sometimes she'd lock herself in the bathroom, and I'd sit alone in the sun on the veranda attached to your bedroom and watch the birds in the yard, or the neighbor move logs to his woodpile, and I'd wait. I'd imagine that you would come back to me as a sunbeam—warm, like you used to make me feel.

I was seven. It was a year after your death. I'd become accustomed to Mom locking herself in rooms with smelly drinks. One spring day, I stayed home sick from school and clung to the toilet bowl for most of the afternoon. My head rested on the porcelain so long it created a half-moon impression on my cheek. Mom stayed home from her job at the florist. It was the first time since you'd died that she took care of me. She made me soup and prepared cold washcloths for my neck to temper the fever. Occasionally, she'd bite her nails and stare at me from the bathroom's entrance as if I'd be sucked into the toilet bowl at any moment, drowned into darkness.

When my stomach settled later that day, she grabbed my hand and led me into the backyard down the brick-path lined with thorny rose bushes. At the end of the path was a bench-swing with an awning.

"Way before your grandfather died," she said, "he and I used to sit in this swing together when I was a little girl. He built it so that, after pruning the roses, he could sit out here with me. Grandma didn't like me staying out here too long. She said little girls shouldn't spend too much time with their fathers."

"How did Grandpa die?" I asked

"How he died is not as important as how he lived," she said.

"How did he live?"

"Loving me."

We sat down on the swing and swayed. Vomit clawed up my throat. I tried to focus on the birds as they sang a strange love song in the cool breeze. The wind teased Mom's hair. She had delicate features and a clear complexion, but that awkward smile. She smoothed her yellow polka-dotted sundress and inched closer to me.

"When I'm gone, you'll do this with your kids."

I picked at my cuticles while a spider needled at a moth caught in its web on a nearby rose.

"Do you love me, Eddie? Tell me you love me."

"I love you, Mom."

Her voice changed, as if someone else spoke for her. "Don't say Mom. Just say you love me."

"I love you."

She leaned over and kissed the corner of my mouth. I could still taste the acid from the vomit.

"My father said that when men grow up and look for a wife, they're looking for their mother. Do you think you'll look for me?"

I didn't know what to say or what she wanted to hear, so I thought of something I had heard you say to her one day in the bathroom as she looked in the mirror at the mascara bleeding down her cheeks.

"Your dress is pretty," I said.

"You're sweet," she said. "I love you, Adam."

She spent time with me, talking to me. It was all a boy could ask for.

We sat there on the swing not speaking, then Mom cried, and I gazed at the pink, red, yellow, and white roses. Butterflies fluttered between the buds, and wasps swarmed in the entrance of a hive under the gutter. I leaned forward and threw up in the grass. Mom rubbed my back and told me that it would be alright, her hand as hot as an oven door.

"You'll feel better tomorrow," she said.

That night, I sat in front of the toilet bowl, wondering what my future wife would be like. I prayed to God for a girl like this version of my Mom who would take care of me when I was sick.

"When you're finished, you can sleep with me tonight." Her pale arms held the frame of the bathroom door. Her shorts had pulled high up her legs, her thighs in need of sun, a church white. Since that day you died, she had slept with her door locked. Some nights I'd wake up from a reoccurring dream of shadow men watching me, and I'd tiptoe to her door and, with only my thumb and pointer, try to turn the rusted knob. It never budged.

I stared into the yellow-stained toilet bowl, cleared my throat, then spit into the water and watched the ripples expand. I flushed the toilet and waved goodbye to my infected spit spiraling into the center and down into the ceramic black hole of the bowl never to return. I felt better already.

4.

Mom often left me with Grandma on the weekends so she could work at the florist. She kept the job for some time after your death. Grandma's house was filled with porcelain, plastic, and crystal. She carried herself with a stiffness. She polished her wooden tables every day with Liquid Gold. Even now, I'll sometimes try to smell something—a flower, perfume, food—but instead, I smell that bitter lemon scent like one of Mom's evening drinks.

Grandma frequently invited her two neighbors, Merma and Darwee, over for canasta and vermouth on the rocks.

"You know, I was a singer, Eddie," Grandma said one afternoon between sips of her drink, placing a card down on the table.

"She was the best," Merma slurred. "The best around."

"Should have heard her," Darwee said.

"Eddie, show M and D your underwear. The ones Grandma bought you for Christmas last year. You're wearing them, right? I told your mother to make you wear them today."

"Yes, Grandma," I said, with that familiar sinking feeling.

"Go and get undressed. When you come back, I'll let you have a sip of Grandma's drink."

I went to the bathroom and stripped down to my underwear. The house was cold, my nipples hard. I lingered in the hallway—an eight year old waiting for something, for someone to come and rescue him.

"Eddie, get in here," Grandma said from her chair. "Dammit,

Merma, you always win." She slapped her cards down on the table.

I walked in front of the three of them with my arms crossed, staring at the cluttered, polished wood shelves that displayed shiny porcelain animals and insects.

"Love the whites," Darwee laughed. She gathered the deck and began shuffling. Her copper hair never moved.

"Just look at that underwear. On sale. Three packs. I'm a good grandmother. I take good care of my Eddo, huh?"

I flinched when she used your nickname for me, like a feigned jab.

"You know that Grandma used to be a singer? Did your mother tell you that?" Grandma said, pausing to take another sip. Her voice sounded like gravel was trapped in her throat. "Sing for me, Eddie. Sing 'Silent Night.'" She slurred the song title. "I taught you that one."

"For God's sake, it's seventy degrees outside. Make him sing something else," Darwee said, dealing the cards.

"He's going to sing 'Silent Night.' That was my favorite." She leaned forward and extended her drink to me. "Sip."

I hesitated, but she pushed the glass closer to my mouth, spilling some of the cold liquid onto my bare foot. I took the oddly shaped glass in hand and sipped. My mouth puckered and eyes watered. It burned my lips, then my throat, like swallowing hot, broken glass.

"Don't you dare spit that out. You swallow it," Grandma said. "Now, sing."

I closed my eyes and sang Silent Night in my prepubescent voice. I pretended I was singing for you, that somewhere you were soaked in orange light, listening to my voice. They laughed. I sang louder. I didn't open my eyes for the entire song. Afterward, they offered me more sips of their drinks.

The next morning, I grew bored and gazed at some of Grandma's collectables while she cut watermelon in the kitchen. She had an old mahogany desk in the hallway displaying different types of statues and figurines. There was a blue and pink butterfly on the second shelf like the ones that flew between Mom's roses in the backyard. It was beautiful and delicate. It beckoned with its fragile antennas: *Come to me. Hold me. Keep me safe in your palm.* I crept down the long hallway and kneeled before the butterfly as if it were God, its fragility, the blend of pastel blues and pinks. Grandma whistled "Silent Night" from the kitchen.

I picked it up. It was cool in my palm. I ran my pointer and middle finger along its smooth edges. The hallway light from behind me illuminated its body, the wings gleamed, and I imagined it flying through cool air toward warm sunlight. Then the light eclipsed. The butterfly was cloaked in shadow.

"What are you doing?"

I turned with the butterfly in my hands.

"What did I tell you about touching my things?"

She reached out to take it from me, but I pulled my hands away. "No," I yelled.

"You little brat."

I gripped the figurine tighter and tighter. It cracked. Then again. Then the sound of the butterfly's last breath—soft—like snow hitting pavement. It collapsed in my hand with a *crunch*. I knew I'd bleed. But maybe that's what I wanted, or for someone to notice me bleeding.

She grabbed me by my t-shirt and opened my hands. The butterfly was in pieces, my blood smeared over each pastel fragment. A sliver of the body was embedded in my palm, and I winced as Grandma plucked it out with little care.

She beat me on my backside, twisting my shirt around her fist with no one to stop her. As hard as I could, I twisted my body around and slammed my elbow into her stomach, screaming, "No, no, stop it!" She hunched forward with the sound of a demon being excised from her body. I ran down the hallway as fast as I could, but she was faster than I thought, caught up to me, clawed at the back of my shirt, and pulled me down the beige tweed carpet, leaving a trail of bloody handprints on the rug.

When Mom picked me up later that day, I heard Grandma tell her about the butterfly, the bloody carpet, my disobedience, the elbow that "nearly killed her" and my "anger problem." This was the beginning of the end. From outside the room, the wicker chair crunched under Mom's fidgeting body.

"It's his father's fault," Grandma said to Mom. "A boy needs a damn father."

"He died, Mom. He didn't leave us. Now what do I do?" Mom said.

"I keep telling you not to coddle him."

"I can't ignore him. He's gone through so much."

"Don't be so dramatic. Did I coddle you after Dad died?"

"But he's all I have."

These words, I've never forgotten. *He's* all I have. He's all *I* have. He's *all* I have. For years, I have twisted the stress of each word in this sentence like a Rubik's Cube to decode its truth.

At eight years old, Mom brought me to my first therapist.

After seeing my first therapist, I was referred to my first psychiatrist.

The psychiatrist referred me to tests. Scantron ovals hardened, solidified, manifested pills before my eyes. The psychiatrist put me on medication with, as the doctor said, "sometimes more side effects than success"—memory loss, insomnia, impotence, dry mouth, dizziness, hallucinations, weight gain, vomiting. And I, too, became a side effect. Every time I visited the psychiatrist, Mom stayed in the room with us. Neither Mom nor the doctor revealed what was wrong with me, why I needed the medication. I assumed it was punishment for my disobedience at Grandma's, the longest punishment in childhood history. By the time I entered middle school, I was on a steady diet of colorful ovals.

Dr. Bleakman sat across from Mom and me in a large leather chair.

"How do you feel today, Eddie?" he asked.

"My stomach hurts."

He looked at Mom. "How do you think he's doing?" He smiled.

What the hell was there to smile at?

"He still cries a lot." She pulled on one of her eyebrows. It wasn't true. At least, I didn't remember crying a lot. "He talks to himself, to things that aren't there." This was true, but only because I was talking to you, Dad.

"I just want—" I started.

"Eddie, you need this medication. Based on what your mother has told me, it would be dangerous for you not to be—"

"But I—"

"Eddie, don't argue with the doctor. Do we have to talk about what happened at Grandma's house?" She turned to Dr. Bleakman. "You see how he gets?"

Dr. Bleakman nodded and closed his eyes. "I want to talk to you about something very important, Eddie. Although you may feel pressured in high school, you can't drink alcohol while taking this medicine. It could be dangerous. Fatal. Do you understand me?"

Mom shook her head in approval. "Thanks."

Dr. Bleakman swiveled in his chair toward Mom. His dark bushy eyebrows rose with his smile. "How's your mother?"

As Mom and Bleakman talked, I glanced around the office. Books on shelves in alphabetical order, a collection of granite heads split in half exposing a brain, neat piles of Post-Its, a name-block in the center: *PhD. Brian Bleakman*, a bobblehead Carl Jung statue, and a bobblehead me sitting across from the doctor. Everything had its place.

5.

I sat on the cracked earth of my front lawn under a pine tree and stared at the ground, stared through it, unable to look away, in a fog as thick as the emptiness in my chest.

"Come on, Eddie," my friend Shane yelled from down the street.

"I don't want to play," I mumbled. I grabbed a handful of dirt, finally emerged from my waking sleep, and threw it into the wind.

Shane rolled his eyes and ran after a group of what used to be my friends passed our neighbor's woodpile.

This was the last time Shane asked me to play with him. He was the last friend I remember having. I had no desire to seek friends, or anything, for that matter, that I once loved, like playing the drums. I feel as if there were fond memories before this, I just can't summon them. I seem to mainly remember ends and entrances.

Mom stood on the other side of our house's glass front door. She put her hand to her pink lips and blew me a kiss, then placed her palm on the door leaving the outline of a deformed print.

A sound tickled my ear. At first, I thought it was the ice-cream truck, but as it got louder, I knew it was something the warm air had carried to me. A white car turned the corner down the street and approached the house. Cars passed our house all the time, but this car moved more slowly, as if searching for an address, or a person. I couldn't see the driver even as the car drew nearer, but I could hear the car's radio, and I could see a dark-haired arm partially covered by a short sleeve bright white t-shirt. Then I heard the lyrics of the song.

"…Maybe I'll catch fire, Something warm to hold me, Something pure to burn away the darkness…"

The song was loud, quick. It tingled at the base of my spine and surged through nerves, extending to the tips of my fingers and toes, finally rising to the surface in the form of goose bumps, hard on my skin like a suit of armor. The distortion of guitars—my guts ripped from my body. The crack of the snare drum—my ribs snapped and fractured. The thud of the bass—memories kicked at the inside of my skull. Then the car and the music were gone. I searched for someone, a *Did you see that?* search, but all I found was an empty street, an ever-widening cracked earth, and a faded handprint on the glass door of my house, an afterimage of where Mom had once been.

6.

The February after I met Elizabeth, I met her mom during a snowstorm that hit Long Island. For some reason, in the middle of the blizzard, her mom needed to go to the local Hallmark store. Elizabeth and I both loved snow, so we didn't mind tagging along.

"So, *you're* Eddie," her mom said before we left. She put her coat on over her Star Trek pajamas.

"Yes, ma'am."

"Don't call me ma'am. Makes me feel old." She zippered her coat and glared at her watch. "Thanks for driving Liz around. It gives me time to relax for once." She grabbed her car keys off the kitchen island and screamed, "Let's go, Liz, I don't have all day. If you're coming, get your ass in here."

We all packed into her mom's four door Chevy Lumina and slid our way through swirls of wind and white gusts. Elizabeth and I clutched each other's coats the whole ride. When we arrived, we exited the car and walked across the virgin snow of the parking lot, our prints covered quickly in our wake. Rare patches of wet blacktop were visible among the white. Our feet crunched on the fresh powder as we held hands and trailed behind her mom bundled in jackets and scarves. We heard each other's thoughts and slowed with the swirling snow as her mom stepped into the store—white lines of suspended time, the wind whistled and swept through the raw air. We found each other's eyes through horizontal flakes. All sound was absorbed into snow, the quietest sound

I can remember—a muted silence.

And then Elizabeth kissed me for the first time. Her tongue grazed my bottom lip, then retreated. She tasted like mint chocolate.

The Hallmark store was littered with people. All were families of three, parents and a daughter or a son. What were they all doing there?

"How gorgeous." Elizabeth's voice rose above the rest. She stared at something in a glass display case.

"What is it?" I asked.

She pointed to a crystal figurine.

The other families stopped and turned to stare with us. It was a horse rearing on its hind legs. She loved riding horses, but I hadn't seen her ride yet. She looked at the statue and appeared to forget this world, forget even me and that I was watching her. What was it like to be lost, to let go? I'd hoped that she would show me.

"I'm going to buy you that," I said.

"No. You don't have to. You don't have money."

She was right. I loved her honesty. "One day, I'll buy you that statue. I promise."

"Alright, we'll see." She brushed my cheek with her woolen fingers.

I closed my eyes.

"Don't you think she'll love it, Eddie?" I heard a voice say from somewhere deep in the store.

"Yes, she will love it. I'll buy it for her one day."

Why Wait? Buy it now? There's never a more perfect time.

I don't have the money.

"But it's her birthday."

When I opened my eyes, I was staring at the crystal horse in a display case, and next to it, Mom held a crystal figurine of a lady singing into a microphone in her palm.

"She can put it on her display table. She had such a beautiful voice. She'll love it. Don't you think?" Her voice trailed off on my name.

In a different display case next to Mom, the same crystal horse

Elizabeth had once admired years before gleamed under a light. The hairs on my arm stood. Everyone in the store slowed like rubberneckers for a roadside crash. They waited for me to say something. Not one person blinked.

"Eddie?" Mom said.

"It's perfect," I said.

"You're not even looking. Did you take your medicine today?"

I looked at the statue in Mom's hand. "It's perfect." But I saw nothing. Clear nothingness. Then Mom's face appeared, distorted through the crystal from its bends and curves. I was numb.

7.

"Eddie, wake up."

"—"

"Wake up, Eddie. It's time."

"Let me be."

"I'll be your eyes."

"What?"

"Open your eyes."

I thought Mom woke me to take my morning dose, but it was Elizabeth. She pulled the covers back from my face and stretched out on her stomach over the white bedsheets. Her blue jeans fell an inch lower, exposing two symmetrical dimples on her lower back.

"Come on, sleepy."

I groaned.

She quietly sang, lay next to me atop the sheets, softened her clear voice to warm me out of bed. *Most relaxing thing I do, hang half way out a third floor window…*"

I knew the song. Somehow I knew it.

"…*maybe I'll fall hard, something tough to break me…*" she continued, then hummed the rest.

"Where have I heard that song?" I asked in a whisper, getting a whiff of my own stale morning breath. The sunlight was on Elizabeth's back, filtering through the French doors from behind her.

"What year is it?" I asked.

She continued humming the familiar song, her eyes closed and her lips pursed. Sunbeams found their way through her hair. "Let's go. You promised we'd go to the bird sanctuary today."

Was this the beginning of our first spring together? It was still cold, but not a winter cold. We put on jackets before leaving.

My car rattled intermittently on the drive to the sanctuary. I gripped the steering wheel tighter, dimpling my hands every time the car shook. You left me your old car in your will. Its color had faded, and it was rusted under the driver's door, but it was yours. And now, it was mine. Sometimes, when I was alone in the car, I would try to smell the seat, the steering wheel, with the hope that I'd smell you, that you'd come back to me as a scent. All I ever smelled was grease and dust.

There were few cars on the Long Island Expressway heading east Sunday morning. Mom enjoyed early mass with Grandma, getting breakfast after service, and then shopping. I was finally old enough to be left home alone. It gave Elizabeth and me hours together. She told her Mom that I was driving her to riding practice—this wasn't always the truth. I told Mom that the medication made me too tired in the morning—this *was* the truth. But waking up early for Elizabeth was like waking up early for Christmas.

The sanctuary is a peninsula on the southern half of the Long Island fork in Sag Harbor. The entrance leading into the small parking lot could easily be missed from the road. My car crunched over gravel as we passed the old, wooden sign for the Elizabeth Morton Wildlife Refuge. There were no other cars in the lot. I found a section of the half-dirt, half-paved lot and parked.

Elizabeth yawned and stretched her arms wide. "It *is* beautiful," she said, looking out the car window at the densely packed trees and different types of birds flying to and from branches.

We exited the car and followed the dirt path to the entrance of the trail.

"What are you doing?" she asked.

"Getting seed," I said, searching my pockets. "The birds are hungry."

We followed the trail over little streams, through puddles and sections of overgrowth. Elizabeth gazed around at the sanctuary like a person from the country walking through New York City for the first time, staring up at maples and out into the reflection of trees and sky in the small lake.

"I can't believe how quiet it is here. My house is so loud when my parents are home. When Mom's home, I should say. Sometimes I wonder how loud my house would be if my parents had any other kids," she said.

"That's why I come here," I said.

"But isn't it quiet enough with just you and your mom?"

"After my dad died, my house became too quiet. Funeral quiet." A bee sting of a headache stung the inside of my head. I wondered if I had taken my medicine before leaving the house? I couldn't remember taking Saturday's night dose either. I saw the colorful pills engraved with numbers atop the kitchen counter where Mom had placed them. *"Don't forget,"* she reminded me at least once daily, as if my heart depended upon them. I closed my eyes and took a deep breath. "That's why I come to this place. Bird songs, wind, trees—these are the noises I want to hear."

I grabbed her small hand and turned it so her palm faced skyward. A circular beam of light marked her open palm as if the sun wished to remind us that we existed.

"It looks like there's a hole in my hand," she said, smiling at me. Her freckles matched the earth.

"I'd better be careful pouring the seed then." Our eyes found each other's as I held her hand open. "I wish I could give you something more than seed," I said. My guts hijacked my body. The sun blinded me. I rubbed my eyes with my fists and stepped back into the shade. The sunbeam painted the bird seed golden in Elizabeth's palm.

"Don't leave me," she said, her voice as thin as communion.

"I'll be right here."

"What do I do if a bird comes?"

"Stay as still as possible."

"I'm not used to being still," she said.

"Try to breathe shallow through your nose. Focus on something that calms you."

"Nothing calms me." Her arm was outstretched.

"What about music?"

"Chopin."

"See, you do have something."

"This place makes me calm."

"Good."

"And you."

The trees were quiet in their movements. They swayed in the wind with a sound like the shuffling of socked feet across wood floors. A bird found a spot next to Elizabeth on a branch, eyeing the food in her palm.

"It's a blue jay," I said in a whisper.

"Is that good?"

"I've never had a blue jay come that close. Stay still."

The blue jay bounced down to a branch even closer to her.

"It's so close," I whispered. "Be careful, blue jays are aggressive."

"Are you kidding?"

"Sometimes they eat the brains of little songbirds and injured birds. Just don't let it near your head." I laughed and covered my mouth with my hand.

"Then it doesn't deserve food. Only nice birds."

"Even mean birds have to eat," I said.

The blue jay hopped from the branch to her hand, a professional thief, grabbing one of the larger seeds, then flew away. "I felt its little legs," she yelled, throwing the remaining seeds in the air, laughing.

It made me smile to hear laughter. "Amazing. I've only had tufted titmice come to me." I moved next to her.

"Where did you learn all that stuff about birds?"

"Apparently my dad. At least, that's what my mom said. He loved coming here with me, especially in the winter."

"You can't remember?"

"Not really." A beach. Your gray eyes. Your hand holding mine. A yellow bird. The fragmented memories existed like the black images Bleakman asked me to interpret. They resembled things I knew, but I didn't know what, why, or how.

Shadows fluttered on the trail as we walked past a pond. Something crackled in the woods. We both turned but saw nothing.

"Why do you come in the winter?" she asked.

"They're starved of food during the winter. They'll put themselves in danger for it. My dad used to say it's like how we crave the sun and warmth during the cold months—"

A wave of nausea swelled and spilled out of me into a pile of leaves. Birds scattered, frightened, but Elizabeth hurried near me, placing her hand on my back between my shoulder blades, and gently rubbing it while humming that familiar song.

"Are you okay, Eddie? Should we head home?"

"I'll be okay. I must have eaten something bad." Only Mom had seen me get sick, seen me this weak, this vulnerable. But Elizabeth stayed with me. She didn't run. She rubbed my back with her cool palm, a balm to my burning body. We stayed there until I felt alright to move on, but the nausea was always a dull ache.

We continued down the path, and the trees on the sides of the trail transformed and darkened. The thick branches above formed a tunnel of trees and eclipsed the sun. The air grew colder. Some of the trees in the park still had no foliage from the winter, allowing the sunlight to creep through the geometric patterns formed by the crisscrossing of branches. The trees thickened as we walked farther. The path dropped every few feet, as if someone had cut giant steps into the earth. Our sky of arching thorny branches enclosed us. I stayed directly in the center of the path.

"Have you ever read Dante's Inferno?" I asked.

"No."

"We read parts of it in English class. There's a section of Hell where Dante meets these tree people. They commit suicide, and so their punishment is to be transformed into these twisted and thorny trees."

"Yummy," she grimaced.

"When Dante breaks a branch off of one, it starts bleeding and telling a story."

"Do you remember any of the trees' stories?"

"Not really. But these trees look like them." I felt nauseous again while thinking of the tree limb breaking off. I swallowed hard, tasting blood, and looked over at Elizabeth.

"Do you think that's what happens when you die? If you kill yourself?" She pulled on her earlobe.

"I don't know. I know I don't want to turn into a tree and not be able to stop other people from breaking my arm off."

"When I was really little, my parents took me to Connetquot State Park. I wandered away from them and found a huge log that I tried balancing on, but I fell into a bush just like those trees. It had thorns all over it. The more I tried to move, the more I got stuck. It was like falling into a bed of toothpicks." She rubbed her forearm as if she could still feel the pain. "I have scars."

She rolled up her coat sleeves and pointed to a few little chicken-pock-like marks on her bronze forearms. They were faint white flecks that shined like pyrite when the sun hit them. I'd never noticed them before because I met her in winter, the season of physical secrets concealed by long sleeves, pants, and coats. It made me wonder what else I hadn't seen, what the rest of her might reveal.

"My parents said they followed my cries. I was a bloody mess. My mom stayed awake with me all that night with a cold towel, wiping my cuts and picking out the rest of the thorns. Or was it my dad? Maybe my dad did that. I think my mom was mad at me for running off in the woods." Her voice softened. I couldn't help wondering if she had fallen off the log or jumped.

We continued down the dark, tunneled path until a glint of beige light appeared in the distance. I remained in the center of the path, Elizabeth close at my side.

When we reached the end of the path, we stopped at the mouth of the beach: a threshold of two realms—half our bodies in beach sun, half still in the thorn tree darkness. The heat of the sun was warm, but the wind was a quick wintery reminder. Elizabeth moved closer to me. There was a small observation deck with a standup binocular machine. Tiny wind ripples rolled from the bay onto the shore in a susurration. Invisible birds chirped faint songs from the trees. The sun spread across the bay in a scad of speckles, like the tiny, shiny scars on Elizabeth's arm. We walked toward the shoreline together, holding hands.

"It looks like the water has goose bumps," she said.

I looked out at the shimmering bay, wondering what, if anything, the water was thinking, feeling.

"My grandpa told me that goose bumps are tiny epiphanies coming to the surface. Maybe the water is having an epiphany right now," she said.

We walked closer to the water's edge. My hand tingled in my pocket around the bag of seed.

"You think the water can sense when something great is happening around it?" she said.

"Right now, I think it knows we're here, and no one else is. I hope it appreciates that."

"I hope so too."

When we reached the shore, we sat down in the sand. Large windowed homes overlooking the water lined the perimeter of the bay. Each home had a dock with a boat. Some boats had sails and others had motors. I thought about my home, our home, our two story split-level. The wood paneling still covering the walls in some of the rooms, paneling Mom would have expected you to peel off, and would expect me to remove and replace with a fresh coat of paint. Did you hope that one day we would be like them, Dad, living in a home of glass, pillars, and marble on the east end? With you gone, it just feels like I'm watching the lives of others from the largest window in the world, wondering just what it all means and why I'm on the inside looking out.

"You think we'll have a home like that one day?" Elizabeth asked.

We. I was already a part of her future. "Probably not," I said. "I don't want a home that big anyway."

"You think you'll live on Long Island forever?"

"I never thought about it. I—I don't know." *He's all I have—He's all I have.* What would Mom do?

"What if I left? I can picture leaving this place with *you,*" she said. "Could you see yourself leaving Long Island with *me?*"

"Why would you want to leave?"

"I don't know."

I could tell she did know. She wasn't joking anymore. Her lips were parted, eyes unblinking and fixed on my mouth as if predicting what I would say before I had said it.

"Can you see yourself leaving this place with me?" she asked again.

"You're fifteen. How can you picture that?"

"You're seventeen. How can you not?"

"I can see myself with you now, here, on Long Island. And I know that—I love you."

I knew I should have felt something when I said this, but I didn't. I wanted to, and I tried to, but I couldn't feel. So I tried to think of the feeling, tried to will it alive until I knew what it was like to at least pretend feeling, to feel not specifically love, but to just feel. She kissed the corner of my mouth, but I turned, worried I still had vomit on my lips. She didn't care. She came in closer. "Kiss me," she urged in a whisper, and kissed me again. Her chapped lips scraped against mine. She rested her head on my shoulder. Something stirred in me, but it remained an ember. We sat there on the beach for a while, staring into the speckled blue of the bay, until a blue flutter darted across us. My head jerked back, and Elizabeth's head fell off my shoulder.

"What's the matter?" she asked.

"Look." I pointed to a beached log in the sand close to the shore. A blue jay sat perched on the log, eating something.

"I've hardly ever seen blue jays. And, since we've been here, we've seen two already," I said. "You must be good luck."

"It's pretty. I'm surprised they're so mean. I wonder if it's the same one."

I leaned forward on my hands and knees. Carefully, I crawled closer to the bird.

"What's it doing, Eddie?" she asked from behind me.

"It's—awful."

She crawled next to me.

The blue jay tore at the thickest of the long red strings of a severed bird head, probably the throat, that was attached to the inside of the head. It looked like melted cheese. The eyes of the head had already been plucked out. The empty sockets fixed on us. I watched as the jay hacked the top of the bird's skull, breaking pieces of it off, exposing the dark pink insides. I gagged a few times. Elizabeth rubbed my back again.

"You okay?" she said.

"I can't seem to look away," I said.

"You're sick."

"If I'm so sick, why haven't *you* looked away?"

"Because—I'm sick too," she laughed, staring at the blue jay. "You were right. They are little shits."

This was the first time I remember her cursing. She may have before, but in the silence, in the moment of watching the bird eat another bird's brains, she seemed human to me. I knew she wasn't human, at least, not fully. It calmed me to think of her as being part human, a demi-goddess, a flawed yet raw quality from this world and the grace and beauty from another. Being in the presence of Elizabeth meant having the ability to see what was coming, what to look forward to both in this life and the next.

"I'm ready to go home, Eddie," she said.

I grabbed her hand and led the way back through the trail, focusing on Elizabeth instead of the thorn trees.

I dropped Elizabeth off at her house. My stomach was still in knots. My car rattled as I pulled up to my house and shut the car off. It was mid-day, and Mom wasn't home yet. I opened the car door and puked on the pavement, a watery, dark liquid. I dropped to the ground, weakened by the heave, and threw up a second time, more liquid, but this time it was clear. My back was burning, no hand for relief. Just me, alone, the biting wind feverishly cold. Old Mrs. Prior, still in her floral nightgown stared at me from her window across the street. I waved, and she retreated into her dark, empty home. I headed inside and swallowed my morning dose of medication that I had missed almost as much as you.

8.

Elizabeth zippered her jacket and moved next to me in the bustle of couples walking out of the movie theatre and into the parking lot.

"It was scary. I don't want to go home," she said.

"What part scared you?" I put my arm around her and pulled her into my body.

"The blood. The music. The murderer was the mom. Everything."

I laughed.

"It's not funny." She stopped walking and stared at me.

"I can't take those things seriously. When they say something is based on a true story before the movie starts, that's when I get a little worried."

She searched the bodies walking out of the theater. We stopped at the front of my car. "You'll protect me, right Eddie?"

"Depends on who's after you."

She smacked me on my chest with her woolen hat, her breath exposed in the cold air.

"Of course I'd protect you," I said.

"What if it was *your* mom after me?"

"That would never happen."

"But what if she was trying to kill me? Who would you help?"

"It's ridiculous."

I walked her to the passenger door and opened it.

"Such a gentleman," she said, stepping into the car. "Thanks, Eddie."

"You're the one who keeps going out in public with me."

It began to rain on the drive to her house. Thick rain drops splattered on the windshield. I turned the wipers and defogger on.

"I didn't think it was supposed to rain tonight," Elizabeth said. She looked in the back seat of my car, her eyebrows raised.

"Me either."

The white road markings faded, blurring the boundary dividing my lane with oncoming traffic. I had driven down the narrow side street before, but never in the dark. Only my headlights illuminated the street.

"It's creepy," she said.

"It's not too far."

"No rush. I feel safer with you than in my own house." She rubbed a spot of her window clean and peered into the night. "When are you coming to dinner? Mom keeps asking me."

"I don't know. Soon."

"The only reason she lets me out with you is so she has some alone time on the weekends when Dad's at work. But she seems more annoyed lately that I've been hanging out so much on weeknights too. And so late. Maybe if she just meets you—"

"I'll come to dinner soon. I promise," I said.

"Does your mom want to meet me?"

"Of course," I said. But I hadn't told Mom about Elizabeth. I had kept her a secret for months. It was the reason I never invited Elizabeth over the house any other time than when I knew Mom would be at church on Sundays, or the few weeknights she worked at the florist.

"I want to meet your mom first," she said.

"Why?"

"I just do. I want to wait for you to come to dinner until after I've met your mom."

"Okay." The rain fell harder. "Did I ever tell you rain is good luck in my family?"

"How so?"

"Not sure. I just remember my mom telling me that. Actually, it's rained on many important events. Kind of sucked now that I think about it."

"Are you trying to make me feel better or worse?"

The car slammed hard over something in the road, the wheel slipped away from me, headlights flashed off something shiny, rain or a street sign, and we skidded sideways. I gained control of the wheel. Then the tires gripped back onto pavement. I pressed the brake and slowed the car to a halt onto the shoulder. My arm had somehow found a rigid path across Elizabeth's chest. She exhaled in a quiver.

"What the hell was that?" she whispered.

"Not sure. You okay?"

"You may have to get this seat professionally cleaned." We forced laughs. "You had to go and talk about the rain being good luck."

"Let me check the car," I said.

Elizabeth grabbed my hand before I stepped out into the darkness.

"What's wrong?" I asked.

She looked at me with wide eyes. "Not sure. Just felt like I needed to do that. To keep you here."

I raised my coat above my head and walked into the night. The rain pelted my jacket. Explosions of water burst off the pavement as if the road were boiling, forming a haze of mist around me. Rain clanged and popped off my car as I crouched in front of each tire, inspecting the rim and tread. Through the haze of water, I found the flat tire, then I noticed Elizabeth's reflection in the side-view mirror. She sat with her hands to her mouth, scanning the darkness in front of the car for a deranged killer, a filicidal mother.

"Flat tire," I said, getting back into the car and closing the door.

"What do we do? How do we fix it?" Elizabeth didn't have her license yet. She knew very little about cars except for how to fill them with gas. There was something rewarding about the prospect of teaching her something, showing her something for the first time. And yet, these moments made me my chest feel hollow. I never had the chance to learn these important lessons from you, Dad. I had to learn how to change a tire from watching a video online of someone else's dad teaching his son how to change a tire.

"I'll have to change the tire. I think there's a spare in the back."

"I'll help you," she said.

"You'll get soaked. Have you ever changed a tire?"

"No, but I'll learn. Let me help."

"Okay. If you really want to."

Then I saw it, a blur halfway down the road. A faded white and blue image shimmering in the rain. Maybe just the splattering of water mixing with the colors of trees, darkness, and headlights.

"What's the matter? Are we going to change the tire?"

"Do you see that?" I asked, staring down the street just past where my headlights no longer illuminated the road, the blur now more distinct.

"See what?"

"I don't know. I just thought—" I cleared some of the fog off the windshield with my sleeve. Now I saw a more distinct figure, a smeared statue in the middle of the street, too far away to distinguish features, but close enough to see the form.

Elizabeth looked down the road. "I don't see anything. That's not funny, Eddie."

She grabbed my hand and squeezed. I kissed her knuckles so hard they knocked against my teeth.

The rain fell harder, faster now. I turned on my wipers, clearing away the rain and the figure. "It was just the rain," I said, not wanting to scare her any longer. Which was more distressing: the fear or the hope?

The rain felt like refrigerated needles hitting my skin. Elizabeth hurried around the car to my side with her jacket over her head.

I went to the back of the car, opened the trunk, then came back around with the spare and kneeled down in front of the flat with the tire iron. Elizabeth raised her face to the sky, blinking as the rain hit her eyes.

She searched up and down the dark street. Shadows expanded in the dark beyond the reach of headlights. I focused on the flat tire.

"We have to loosen these bolts first. Then jack the car."

She crouched beside me. Even through the rain, her breath warmed my cheek with a buttery brush. "Can I try?" she asked, already grabbing the metal cross from my hands.

"It's raining. I'll just show—" Before I finished the sentence, she had already loosened the first bolt. That excitement of wanting to teach her was quickly eclipsed by a bottomless fear of extinction that swelled at the base of my guts.

The rain slowed to a drizzle. "Oh, I didn't think you'd—" I began.

"I'm stronger than you think," she said, then paused after seeing my face. "I'm sorry, did I steal your job?"

"No. It's fine." I stepped back and watched Elizabeth loosen the bolts, one by one. I swallowed the ancient foolishness and grabbed the jack from the back of the car.

"You're a guy's dream, you know that?" I said.

"What do you mean?"

I lay on the wet ground, positioned the jack, and began propping up the car. "You're beautiful, thoughtful, and you change tires."

She smiled and moved a chunk of wet hair from her forehead. "What's next?"

I cranked the jack until the side of the car was off the ground. "Now we take the bolts and tire off."

She didn't move for a moment. Her eyes were fixed on a puddle of black water. The rain vanished. The chill remained. "Eddie, when do you think you'll die? Like, how old you think you'll be?" Water rushed into a nearby street drain.

"How did we get on this topic?" I took the flat tire off.

"You think it'll be painful? Did you see the son's face when he was stabbed?"

We kneeled in prayer position next to each other on the quiet, wet street. I placed the new tire on the axle and began hand-tightening the bolts.

"That's a movie. But I'd imagine it's painful. I mean, you're dying, so it must hurt. Depends how you die."

"How did your dad die?"

I swallowed the question like metal tacks. "Car accident. Driving home from work."

"Did he fall asleep?"

"I don't know. My mom and I never really talked about it. We just kind of kept living."

"What did he look like?"

"Brown hair. Always wore a white t-shirt and blue jeans. Gray eyes."

"Like yours."

"I guess. I think his were lighter. Grayer."

"Your mom must miss him. I'd miss you if you died."

I stopped tightening the bolts and looked up into the sky, then up and down the street seeing only more darkness.

"Can we talk about something else?" I said.

Her eyes were steady on me. "I'm sorry. I don't mean to pry." Then she said, "That's a lie. I did mean to pry. I just want to know everything about you."

I grabbed her greasy hands in mine, her face dark in the shadows. "I'm sorry."

"It's okay. The idea of just, I don't know, not existing, scares me. And when I'm scared, I have to talk about what scares me. It really annoys my mom. I'm not too good at the whole death thing."

It began to drizzle. A siren sounded somewhere in the distance. I released her hands and looked down the dark road again expecting to find police lights.

"Everybody dies," I said.

"It makes me sad that I'll be forgotten one day. You said you can hardly remember your father."

"I was young and—" And I almost revealed my secret, the medication. It didn't feel like the right time to tell her. Not yet. "Who could forget you?" There was grease on her larger earlobe. I didn't tell her.

"Why wouldn't they forget me? I'm just some average girl from Farmingville, Long Island. My family barely remembers me."

"I won't forget you. I don't have any friends. My mom and I are, well, we don't really talk about normal stuff. You're all I have." With sudden clarity, I knew how Mom felt when she had uttered the very same phrase years ago. It wasn't entirely true though. I had Mom too. But it didn't always feel that way. It felt more like Mom had me more than I had her.

Then Elizabeth kissed me, and for only a brief moment, she slipped her salty tongue into my mouth.

I quickly finished tightening the last bolt on the tire and looked at my watch. "Hey, it's Ash Wednesday."

"God, I haven't been to church since Christmas of last year. Aren't we supposed to get those crosses on our foreheads?"

I raised my greasy thumb to her forehead. "In the name of the father, and of the son, and of the holy spirit," I said, and made a tire-grease-cross on her forehead.

She laughed and concluded the ceremony with an "Amen."

"Let's get this busted tire in the back and get in the car before it starts to rain again."

I started the engine and turned the heat on high. "I have a towel in the back seat," I said, watching Elizabeth wipe rainwater from her face with her forearm. She was trembling.

She turned around and reached between the two front seats and into the back. Her thigh pressed against my arm, and I let myself lean into her. She found the towel and returned to her seat. She wiped her face, hands, neck, and hair. A bead of rainwater ran down her jaw, curved under her chin, and vanished into the dark hollow of her chest. "Here, dry yourself off. I only used this section." She placed the towel on my lap. Her hand lingered on my thigh for a moment, then slowly retreated.

"Thanks," I said. We caught each other in an awkward stare.

"Elizabeth, I—"

"It's been—"

More silence. Then smiles. The car warmed.

"Go ahead," I said to her.

She wanted to say something. Was it what I was thinking but couldn't feel? Was it the fear and the warm tingling rising with the heat in the car and the hypnotic hum of rain pattering against the windshield, the feeling bleeding back into my hands and feet and the rest of my body, and her body, her chest's naive curves, crevasses, and other pockets of unexplored darkness? My mind was shuffling through possibilities, but my chest remained cold—numb.

"I—" she paused. "Thank you for teaching me how to change a tire."

We drove home in silence. I thought about Elizabeth's thigh, what shade of white it might be. I caught her staring at my unsteady hands, another side effect. I gripped the steering wheel tighter.

"If there is a God," she said, "a place we go after—I want to see you there." The words came from her mouth like a song that had been sung to her throughout childhood.

I took my eyes off the road and looked at her, still digesting the words. "That would be something," was all I could muster.

We arrived at her house, the neighborhood quiet and the air misty.

"What were you really going to say before?" I asked.

"I told you."

"No you didn't."

"What were you going to say? You didn't say what you were going to either," she said.

"In case there is no heaven—"

She shifted her body closer and pressed her mouth to mine. There was a slip of her tongue again on my top lip, then much deeper into my mouth. My world spun, and she whispered something incomprehensible into my ear. Her tongue touched my teeth, tapping memories, years of loneliness and fear. I worried what she would find, what I would find between her chest, and deeper into darkness, into my darkness, a hollow place, an afterglow of a childhood without a father. Her hand moved low, I shifted, she groaned, I moved, she moaned, I prayed for warmth but found only cold. "Is it me?" she asked. But really she meant, *"It's me."* No, Dad, it wasn't her, but the meds. It was Mom. It was even you—"I'm cold," I said, the black grease-cross luminous on her forehead. "I'm numb," I said to the undefined shadows of my room, drinking my night dose with cold water, lying in an even colder bed. Did I speak the words?

She was with me once—like grief. But you, Dad, never again.

9.

Mom's heartbeat was slower than Elizabeth's. More of a funeral march than a spring etude.

Thum-thum, thum-thum, thum-thum.

My eyes were open, dark hues of pinks and reds. Warm music. Smooth as the walls of the womb.

Thum-thum, thum-thum, thum-thum.

Mom's voice, sweet, out of time with her heartbeat, singing muffled words of a melody.

Thum-thum, thum-thum, thum-thum.

Submerged in warmth and music, a slick voice without a face, a goddess I worshiped but could not see. But I could not stay forever. I had to be brought forth to life and know my creator. And know.

Thank

God for Elizabeth.

Thank

God

for

her.

10.

Mom sat at the kitchen table by the window reading a *Catholic Digest* one morning when I told her about Elizabeth for the first time.

She raised her head from reading and paused. "That's why you've been acting strange lately?"

"I didn't know I was acting strange," I said.

"A mother knows when her son isn't right." She remained still for a few moments. "Did you tell her about your medicine?"

"No, and I want to keep it that way."

"If she doesn't accept you for who you are, then—"

"It's not who I am."

"Then what is it?"

"I don't think I need it."

"Let's not go through this again. Remember Grandma's house? The butterfly? You hurt your grandmother, Eddie. You—"

"Just do me a favor, don't tell her about it, okay?"

"Does this mean she's coming over?"

"She wants to meet you."

"She can come. I'll make meatloaf. But I won't make promises."

It was not the right time to tell Elizabeth about the medication. I was still waiting for that right moment. For once, it would have been a relief to extinguish the burning ember that glowed in the center of my chest.

When Elizabeth came to dinner, we all sat around the table together: Elizabeth on my right, Mom on my left—I was the center.

"It's so great to finally meet you," Elizabeth said. "Eddie's told me so much about you."

The house was quiet, the kitchen dimly lit. Mom didn't respond. She didn't even look at her. She just cut the meatloaf on her plate. Elizabeth tugged at her larger earlobe.

"Smells delicious," Elizabeth said.

All I could smell was Grandma's Liquid Gold.

Mom picked up the bowl of yams and served me two spoonfuls. "I hope you like it, Eddie. I made this just for you. I know how much you love it."

"Thanks, Mom," I said.

"Can I have a scoop, please?" Elizabeth asked, lifting her plate toward Mom.

Mom set the bowl of yams down in front of Elizabeth who still had her plate suspended in air. Elizabeth set her plate down, grabbed the spoon, and began to scoop a spoonful out of the bowl.

"Sweetie, are you sure you want that?" Mom said.

Elizabeth furrowed her brow and held the serving spoon steady above the bowl. "What do you mean?"

"Well," Mom began, "with all those new studies, how carbs make you gain weight." She paused to take a bite of her meat.

Elizabeth was petite by anyone's standards, but she placed the spoon down as carefully as she could. "Maybe just a small bite, then. Thank you."

Two carrots and a piece of meatloaf were drowning in mashed yams and gravy on my plate. I could only save the meatloaf in time. The grandfather clock's ticks hammered, echoed, throbbed with my headache. I ate another piece of meat. Elizabeth's perfume reached my nose. I had never known her to use perfume before, strong and almost acidic, or maybe that was still the Liquid Gold. Her bangs were somehow tucked neatly under another part of her hair. A blue butterfly hair clip held it all together.

"Eddie tells me you garden?" Elizabeth said.

Mom placed her fork down. "Yes?"

"He said your roses are beautiful. Could you show me some time?"

"Do you know anything about roses?"

"I love their smell. I bought perfume that smells like them."

"That's what that smell is," Mom said softly.

Silence again.

"Elizabeth's dad is a chef," I said to Mom.

"Did you tell her that your father was a cop?"

"Yes," Elizabeth said. "And I'm sorry for your loss." The response was a bit too eager. The poor girl tried so hard.

Mom placed her fork down on the table, sighed, and rubbed her temples with both hands as if attempting to abate a headache. "Elizabeth, what grade are you in again?"

"I'm in ninth, but I'm one of the oldest in my class."

"Do you know what it's like to be in love?"

Elizabeth's face pinched, trying to understand and deciding how to respond.

"What is your idea of love?" Mom asked her.

The three of us sat in a triangle at the small round kitchen table. Under the table, a foot rubbed the inside of my left leg, up then down.

"I love Eddie," Elizabeth squeaked. "I don't know how I know, I just do."

I smiled. Then the foot retreated from my leg.

"Let me tell you about love," Mom said. "We were in 11th grade. His name was Adam, Eddie's father. High school sweethearts. You know the odds of that working out? We did. We defied the odds. We were both in the chorus. He came to school very ill on the day of our concert." Mom turned to me. "Grandma told me she knew what talent was, and that I didn't quite have it. She was right. She was a good singer before her throat surgery, to remove that tumor. She did know talent, I'll give her that. But I wanted her to come to at least one of my concerts. Just one." Mom refocused on Elizabeth who now looked like a firefly trapped in a glass jar.

"I stood on the risers with the rest of the singers, and right before we were about to sing, I saw Grandma all the way in the back of the auditorium with her arms crossed. Imagine that. She came to my concert. I couldn't believe it. But just before singing the opening song—" Mom paused, looking into a pile of mashed meat, gravy, and yams on her plate.

"What happened?" I asked.

"Chaos. Your dad puked. Students were running in all directions. I ran to your father and sat next to him in front of a pile of his own vomit that had gone through the gaps in the risers to the floor. Students had walked in it, traipsing it into the crowd, while we sat on the top of the risers, the only ones left. What a catastrophe. The only show my mom came to and—vomit."

"What did you do?" I asked. Mom had never told me so much of her childhood before.

"I needed to fix it, somehow," she continued. "So I sang Grandma's favorite song, 'Silent night, holy night. All is calm, all is bright.'" Mom sang right there at the dinner table as if lulling a baby to sleep. Her voice reminded me of Grandma's fragile, iridescent capiz shell chandelier.

"I sang with my arms around your father, staring at my mom. And you know what your grandmother was doing, Eddie?"

I shook my head.

"Laughing. She was laughing. What did that mean? Was she enjoying it, or just laughing at me? I didn't care. She was there and wasn't leaving. That's what mattered. So I kept singing to the end of the song, vomit stench and all. And then, as if your father somehow sensed how upset I was, he joined in on the last lines. 'Sleep in heavenly peace.' The janitor wheeled a mop and bucket down the center aisle. All the parents and kids just stared at the two of us, except my mom who was in the back, in the dark, laughing so hard she cried. 'Sleep in heavenly peace.' Your father finished singing the last line with me."

Elizabeth wasn't looking up any longer. She was moving food around on her plate. And it was just as well. Mom seemed to have forgotten Elizabeth was even there, or that she was telling a story. She looked around the room as if searching for you, Dad. Then she stared across at Elizabeth and remembered where she was. "Do you want to know what love is?"

Elizabeth tried to vocalize a "yes," but it was lip-synced.

"Love is singing the last line together."

Elizabeth never asked to eat at my house again. I never asked her to, either.

It was a quiet car ride that night back to her house. She gave me a quick kiss on the corner of my mouth and fled into the darkness of her home. I thought our relationship was over. I waited for the call that night to tell me she couldn't date a kid with a mom like mine. That I had lured her to dinner without warning and let Mom embarrass her. I never got the call. It was as if it never happened.

When I arrived home from dropping Elizabeth off, I went to Mom's room.

"Eddie, come sit down next to me," Mom said. I did.

She let her brown hair down from her bun. The moon shone through the French doors on the other side of the room. The neighbor's woodpile glowed outside like an anchored star. Mom's hair swallowed the moonlight in the room.

"What was that at dinner?"

"I'm not sure she's mature enough to understand you, or love, for that matter. If she doesn't love you for you, for us—" She handed me her hairbrush. "Can you brush my hair tonight? Just for a little while. Your father would sometimes do it for me before we'd fall asleep."

In smooth strokes, I brushed. I didn't know whether to brush her hair, break her neck, or brush her hair so hard it would break her neck. Her hair always seemed so soft in the light from afar. It was as coarse as steel wool when I touched it. She opened her nightstand drawer and pulled out a bottle of cream.

"Since your father died," she said, "I only have you and Grandma." She cried while rubbing the cream on her face, avoiding her cheeks so the cream wouldn't bleed. "Let's enjoy the time we have together."

I traced her neckline with my eyes, down to her clavicle where a small pocket formed, where I hid until Mom told me I was finished.

After she went to bed, I went into her liquor cabinet and stole a small, half-empty bottle of Jack Daniels. I washed down my night dose of medication with the whisky, disregarding Dr. Bleakman's warning because—fuck Bleakman. Even if I rejected the boy Bleakman, Grandma, and Mom thought I was, I didn't have any other version of me I could replace him with. The only other form of me I could remember was before the medication: sad, lonely, angry. But in a way, Mom was right. I would never know if Elizabeth truly loved me until she knew who I was or what I had become after you died.

I walked around the block of my neighborhood, drank half of the booze, cried, then puked. I finished the bottle, cried some more, and puked again. I wanted to rip out of my skin and crawl my raw, bloody body the length of the Long Island Expressway.

The local elementary school's playground was nearby, so I went there and climbed on a giant slide. Sitting at the top, I looked down into the sand. The ground moved in waves with my nausea. Looking at the sky was gazing into a kaleidoscope and twisting the tube. I prayed Elizabeth wouldn't leave me. Then I prayed for you, Dad. Nothing specifically, just for your presence—to know you. "Fuck you," I yelled to the stars.

I slid down the slide and hit the sand at the bottom. There was movement in the darkness ahead of me. My drunkenness. My memories. The darkness collapsing around me, on me. Two shadows crisscrossed, moved rapidly toward me. I ran. Puke sprayed from my mouth. Balance beams, jump. Sand box, jump. But the growling beasts tackled me.

11.

I was in the driver's seat of my car, always in that car. Elizabeth leaped out of her house, around the front of my car, and opened the passenger's door.

"You're late," she said smiling.

"As always."

"Happy anniversary. We've been dating six months today." She closed the door.

I backed out of her driveway. "You're right. I feel like I've known you longer," I said. "Do you remember when I first met you? When I had—"

"The mohawk? You didn't have to—"

"Shave it? Yes I did. I wanted to. For your mom. For you."

She turned and scanned my face with an eyebrow raised. Then she smiled. "I like your cute, short hair now, anyway." She ran her hand through my hair. "How do you have blonde hair anyway? Didn't you say your dad had brown hair? And your mom has brown hair too."

"Maybe a recessive trait."

She smiled and closed her eyes as she pulled on the seat lever and reclined it a few inches. "You know, I've never been with someone this long. Never had anyone want to be around me as much as you do," she said.

"I think it's your name."

"My name?"

"Your name is a name that people fall in love with. Anytime you watch a movie, the guy falls in love with a girl named Elizabeth."

"Name one movie," she said.

"I can't really think of any right now." It felt true, nonetheless.

We held hands the entire car ride. By the time we reached the stable, our hands were clammy with anticipation. I wiped my shaky palms on my jeans. Elizabeth ran toward the stable. I waited on some haystacks near the cherry blossoms. The sun had risen, warming everything with its breath.

"How do I look?" She was sunshine atop a horse. Her thighs pressed tightly around the horse's sides—to be that horse. A black riding helmet covered her head, but her hair came down the sides of her face barely touching her shoulders. A few bangs escaped the cap and stuck to her eyelashes.

"You look like one of those Greek sculptures you see in history books," I said, using my hand as a visor.

Elizabeth dismounted, guided her horse to a post near the pen, and tied it up. "I have a gift for you. For our six month anniversary," she said.

"You didn't have to—"

"I needed to. I want you to have it." Elizabeth sat down next to me.

I moved away from her and sat on the ground.

"You don't want to sit next to me?"

"It's not that. I just—I like to look up at you. Especially with the sun behind you."

She scrunched her nose and tossed her brown hair off her bronze neck. "You give me too much credit, Eddie." She took out a small wooden box. "I wanted to get you something that you'd remember." Elizabeth looked away from me as if listening to a song I couldn't hear.

"Are you okay?" I asked.

She refocused. "I wanted to get you something that would help you, like you've helped me. Something that, when you look at it, you'll remember all the times we spent together. But also something that makes you smile. I'll just give it to you. I'll probably ruin it if I talk about it too much. Here." Elizabeth extended the box to me. Her tiny forearm scars shimmered on her skin like brown beach glass. "I borrowed money from my mom. She's good for something," she said with a transient smile.

"I want you to open it for me," I said.

"No. You have to open it."

"Please. I want to watch you open it. I won't remember it the way I want to if you don't take it out of the box."

"You're so odd. But I love that." She pulled the box back and placed it on her lap. "I hope you like it."

She opened the box and exhaled light. Slowly, she held up the sun that dangled from a gold chain and let it light the world around me, in me. Spit stuck in the back of my throat, and I fumbled for words. The freckles on her nose danced with the windblown dandelions, and her gift of light swayed and spun from her fingers.

"You look like something I'd like to see when I die," I said.

She giggled, turned her face toward the cherry blossoms, then closed her eyes as a breeze ran across her face. "If I got that remark from anyone else, I'd think it was a threat."

"If there is an afterlife, I hope I see you there, the way you look right now. I—can't speak."

"You're doing fine," she said. "Do you know what it is? It's a pocketwatch. Here, read the inscription."

She handed me the watch, and I read the outside:

To my love,
There is always enough time.

"It's—" I stumbled.

"Do you like it?"

"I—"

"It's okay. You don't have to say anything. I knew you'd love it. I told you that my biggest fear is that people won't remember me. Now, I just want *you* to remember me. If I could have that, I can be happy," she said.

I held the pocket-watch by the chain and let it reflect sunlight onto her chest as it spun in the wind. "This will always bring me back to you. I'll always remember."

I know what you were expecting, but some memories are good. They are simply good. Nothing less. This is my good memory. Let me have this memory.

12.

"Eddie?"

"Who is this?"

"Mom."

"Doesn't sound like you."

"You'd think you'd know my voice by now, and I thought that after getting you a cell phone you'd check in with me more often."

"I'm sorry."

"Grandma and I just got home from church. I need your help. A light burned out in the hallway. I don't want to fall off a chair replacing it."

"I should be home in another hour or so."

"An hour? What are you doing? I can't see without the light. You know I hate being in the dark."

"Mom, can't I—"

"I'm not feeling well. I'm sick today. I feel dizzy. I can't change the bulb myself. How would you feel if I fell off a chair trying to replace it?"

"I'll be home in fifteen. I'll talk to you later."

"You didn't say I love you. Don't ever get off the phone without saying I love you. What if something happens?"

"I love you, Mom."

"Just say I love you."

"I love you."

13.

I went to the local craft store and bought some materials. It was nearing the end of my 11th grade year, a couple months before the summer. But it was Friday night, which gave me a little over two full days to create whatever it was I was going to create with a block of clay, paint, and tools I had never seen before.

"I'll be in the basement, Mom." I ran through the front door and downstairs. There were two Eddies: one obligated to Mom, the other devoted to Elizabeth.

"Wait a sec. You haven't taken your medi—" Mom's voice disappeared as I vanished into the basement study.

The basement was the only place Mom avoided. Her reasons may have been the same as mine. But I knew I could work quietly and alone without distractions. I had not been down there since the months that followed your death. There was something disturbing about going below the surface, whether it was walking down the stairs or digging my hands too far in the earth.

But now, there was only the tip of a surge, the edge of a warm rush of excitement in my bones, a feeling I couldn't remember feeling. My fingers tingled like two slabs of meat thawing in sun. A secret mission. A divine undertaking. I didn't want to ruin the table with paint and clay, so I grabbed a handful of newspapers I found piled in the corner. As I laid out my materials, a newspaper article fell to the floor. It had been torn out already. I picked it up. The 1986 news article read, *"Nassau*

County Cop Dies in LIE Wreck." I remained still. A coincidence. Just a coincidence. I moved the box of clay and read. It was the article written after you died. How? Where did it come from? Why was this newspaper still here? Had Mom kept it all this time, buried in an underground corner? My eyes darted around the room expecting to find you. That surge I had felt moments ago ebbed. *Cop dies driving home...unknown driver error...legacy of excellence...survived by...survived by...his wife and...his wife, Brenda, and...child, Eddie, Eddo...Survived by his child, Eddie.*

I survived.

Knocks at the door.

"Eddie?"

More knocks. I stayed quiet.

"Eddie? You in there? You didn't take your medicine this morning. You missed last night's, too." I heard her rusty head turn, the faint press of her fleshy ear against the door. Her breath was heavy, as if the air was thicker in the basement. I imagined her scanning the dark passage leading to the door, searching for a disembodied voice. "You can't take all of those doses at once. You have to space them out," she said. "Eddie, I know you're in there."

"No, I—I just replaced the pills after I took them." I couldn't remember.

"You've never done that before. Are you sure?"

"Yeah."

"What are you doing in there?"

"Working on something—for you."

"Oh. Okay. Sorry."

I heard her hand slowly slide down the door. Then footsteps back upstairs. I felt the guilt again. Though, had I not taken last night and today's doses, I would be feeling a lot more than guilt in a few hours, like the time at the bird sanctuary when I puked in front of Elizabeth.

I sat down with the tools on my left, a cup of water to my right, and all the paints spread out like a priest at his altar preparing for communion. At the center of the table, a block of clay. It felt more like a project now. I doubted my ability to shape it into anything. I took a creased picture of Elizabeth out of my pocket. She stood next to her horse, held the reins. Her other hand rested on the horse's forehead. The leaves on the trees next to the barn were red and yellow, and her smile was white. Her mouth's a black hole, as if a joke had just been told. I laid it next to your news article. My muses: Elizabeth and—your death. Can death be a muse?

It was easier to think of creating something beautiful than to actually create beauty. Had God felt this way before creating us?

Friday:

7:45pm: I spent the first hour staring at the clay. For about ten minutes, I thought the clay might form itself into Elizabeth. I looked at your news article and read it a few times over, hoping to find some clue as to who you were until I slammed my fist down on the clay.

8:30pm: I fell asleep and was awakened by Mom at the door.

"Eddie, open up. I know you're in there. Why are you ignoring me? Eddie? What are you doing?"

"I'm still working on it."

"Fine, but unlock this door. You haven't taken your night dose. You're going to be sick if you don't."

"I'll be out in a little while."

"You've been down here almost an hour."

"I'll be out later." But I wasn't.

9:30pm: I snuck upstairs when I heard Mom's bedroom door shut and grabbed a box of Cheez-Its and a two liter bottle of diet cream soda. I raced back downstairs, locked the door of the study behind me, uncovered the crafts, and sat down at the table only to stare at the clay again.

I recited a few Hail Marys followed by The Lord's Prayer. I made an uneven cross out of the clay then rolled it back into a ball. Mom told me we used to go to church every Sunday together, as a family, but I could never seem to remember this.

I said a few more Hail Marys. *When in doubt, pray to the Virgin Mary.* Who told me this? "Now and at the hour of...Now and at the hour..." The words were trapped in my chest. I picked up the news article of your death. *Now and at the hour of your death...My death...Our Death...Amen.*

11:00pm?: Little clay men kept me from sleeping. They grew into larger men, darker figures with wings and long tongues. They crowded the table and tugged on my fingernails. But the Virgin Mary appeared from the cup of water and broke the dark clay with her palms of light. She warmed my chest but didn't speak. She didn't have to.

Saturday

3:03am: I woke feeling hungover. Something burning. I thought I would find a fire in the room. I unlocked the door and walked upstairs. Mom was snoring in her room in a bed too big for one. In the kitchen, all of the appliances were off. Mom left the kitchen table light on, so I pulled the cold lamp chain and sat in the dark. Three doses of my medicine lay out on the table in front of me. I had missed three doses already, not including the morning dose I would have to take today. I let my hands rest next to the pills on the cool wood table. The grandfather clock in the living room ticked. I picked up the pills and saw Mom's face in each oval. *"You'll get sick."* And yet, so far, after three missed doses, I felt no serious signs of sickness like the last time. So I threw them in the garbage pail next to me and laid some napkins on top so that Mom wouldn't see them.

Everything was shadows. The burning smell had weakened, yet still it clung to things. It wasn't really a burned food smell. It was more like burned rubber. Then the house creaked. *"The creaking sounds are signs of the house still settling."* Another misplaced memory. Another creak. This time louder. This time from within. Maybe my ribcage was finally settling. How long does it take to settle, Dad?

5:25am: I fell asleep at the kitchen table. When I awoke, the sky was the color of one of those dark blue urinal cakes. The midnight blue glow broke through the kitchen window and painted my right shoulder. I could hear Mom snoring louder than before. Did she always snore that loudly? Did it keep you up at night like it does me?

The burning smell was gone. I went into my room and fell asleep in my bed. I had a dream the house caught fire and my bedroom door was locked. The Virgin Mary never came.

9:10am:

"Time to get up, Eddie," Mom yelled from her bedroom.

I opened my eyes under the comforter, wrapped in sweat-soaked sheets. I took a shower, brushed my teeth, and went into the kitchen. I sat in the chair I had fallen asleep in. The table light I had shut off was on again.

"Mom, did you come into the kitchen this morning?"

"No. Still in bed. Be up soon."

"No, it's okay."

"Did you take your meds last night? Don't forget to take this morning's dose."

"Yes. And I know." Why hadn't I puked? Three doses? The most missed so far, and yet, all I had was a slight headache and the always unsteady hands. I was so preoccupied with my clay creation for Elizabeth. Forgetting to take my medicine had not been a deliberate decision. It was instead like a river changing course because the earth makes it so.

I pulled the lamp chain with my trembling hand, turning the light off, and went back down to the study.

9:30am:

My freckles, Eddie. Don't forget my freckles, Elizabeth called from her photo. Sometimes when you look for beauty in a person, you notice something that prevents them from being beautiful. But with Elizabeth,

I struggled to find a flaw. And even if there was a flaw, I knew her. All her little nose scrunches and sweet nuances. I wouldn't see her flaws even if there were any. But there weren't.

Hungry, I went back upstairs without creating a single impression in the clay.

Some moments are meant for admiration.

11:00am: I saw eyes in the bowl of Cheerios. Tiny white eyes, staring, waiting for me to create, to mold and shape the smooth edges, the clay braid down her back, the soft hand on the horse's forehead. *"You don't need to eat. You think she'll wait forever?,"* the Cheerios said. I'd hoped so, but I wasn't taking any chances. I didn't need to give her any more reasons to not want to be with me, especially after the awkward dinner with Mom weeks ago, and even more so, because I was planning on telling her about my medication. It was just a matter of waiting for the right moment.

11:28am: I shaped a solid base, then built more on top. The structure narrowed as it ascended, tower-like. I tore a piece of clay from the large base and broke it into many little balls. I rolled each little ball out into spaghetti-like strips and attached them to the base of the clay, bending the strips into different directions. I ripped another piece off the clay base, shaped it into a perfect circle and attached it to the top of the statue. When I finished, it resembled a tree with a human head. I destroyed it and poured a drink of diet cream.

1:52pm: I worked, looking down at the picture of Elizabeth, eating a Cheez-It, wiping my forehead with my arm, using all the tools I'd bought at the store, but probably for different purposes than originally intended. I worked in sections: the arms, the horse, the body. I wanted to destroy any part of her that didn't come out the way it should, the way I had imagined it would. Mold, shape, water, shape, knead, roll, blend, knuckle. My hands were gray, and my mouth had an artificial sweetener aftertaste from the diet soda.

9:12pm: Mom never came down to check on me. I couldn't tell if she was home. I had one thing in mind, and stopped only for a moment to look at how far I had come: a smooth base, a pair of unattached arms, some strands of hair, and an undefined head. The pieces of wet clay looked glassy under the halogen desk light. Elizabeth's unpainted gray head was nothing more than a wet stone. My eyes burned from being open so long and wide. I stopped what I was doing and closed them. When they opened, tears rolled down the sides of my face. My head was heavy. I laid it on the table and slept.

Sunday

3:32am: I jumped from the top of a building and fell into a thicket of thorn bushes. A shadow lit them on fire, and I felt the heat, smelled the burning of wood. I heard the crackling of flames. It was the crackling that woke me.

I was in the basement. Something was burning. I expected to see a fire, to hear screams and flickers of light. The smell was so strong I could taste the burn, a chalky charcoaled taste.

In the kitchen, at first nothing seemed unusual, but the smell was even stronger. I checked all the appliances but found only stovetop grease stains and dirty plates next to the oven. I spotted six doses of medication on the kitchen counter. Had Mom found them in the garbage? Some of the pills had coffee grinds stuck to them, a dab of ketchup on another pill, and one pill was wet and slowly dissolving on the counter. I threw them in the garbage again. The clock ticked.

The kitchen table lamp had been left on again. The scent grew stronger as I walked down the hallway to Mom's bedroom. I put my shirt over my mouth and nose. Her door was shut. All those times as a kid after you died, checking on her, making sure she hadn't left or died too. Mom must have felt the same, worried I would have left her without saying goodbye.

The stench permeated every inch of the space outside her room. I put my ear to the door. I didn't hear snoring. The door's handle was warm.

Dead? Her body engulfed in flames? Or maybe missing altogether? I'm an awful son, Dad, because for a moment I felt something like relief. She wouldn't be my responsibility. Elizabeth and I could leave, go to college, out of state somewhere, with no one to worry about but ourselves. I would grieve, I'm sure, but I was a professional griever.

Instead, when I opened the door, I saw Mom sleeping quietly. I walked closer to see the rise and fall of her chest, just to be sure. The smell dissipated. When it cleared, a sweet scent lingered—roses.

8:49am: I awoke in my own bed. Mom was at church, as usual. I had a headache from the smell and a neckache from sleeping on tables the past few nights, but I still didn't feel nauseated.

I got to work, yet again, rolling shapes, pressing, smoothing edges, and sometimes admiring the likeness to the photo. While forming the forehead of the horse with a tiny shovel, I sliced my pointer finger open over the clay. The dark red ran down the sides and over the water-slickened sections of gray statue, seeping into clay cracks and separations. I wiped off what I could, not wanting to destroy my work to extract the blood.

4:25pm: I stopped to eat stale Cheez-Its and flat soda. One of the stale Cheez-Its cut the roof of my mouth, and I bled. I kept one piece of paper towel in my mouth to absorb the blood and another wrapped around my finger. Who knew clay was so dangerous?

"Eddie?"

I stopped shaping the clay.

"Eddie, are you still in there? I think it's great you're making me something. But I'd rather spend time with you," she said from the other side of the locked door.

"I know. But I'm almost done, Mom."

"Okay." There was a pause. "Eddie, did you take your medicine this morning? The doses were missing on the table upstairs. Remember what I said. You can't take them all together. You'll get sick."

"I know."

"Let me know when you're finished. You have school tomorrow."

"Okay, Mom."

"Love you."

"Love you too, M—I love you too."

7:00pm: I assembled Elizabeth and the head of the horse. It was somewhat abstract. I realized halfway through that I didn't have enough clay for the entire body of the horse, so I only created the head. Elizabeth's entire body was as big as the horse's head.

I finished within the hour. I put everything together. Despite my doubts, it came out quite good. I painted the statue and sat for a while admiring the creation glistening under the lamp, the clay wet from the paint like a creature from the sea. It was the size of a large soup mug. Elizabeth's hand rested on the white diamond of the brown horse's forehead, her dress pink, a slight deviation from the picture, and a yellow flower placed in her brown hair. All that was left to do was cook the statue, fire it so that it would harden into a permanent fixture. But it would take hours, and I would have to wait until Mom was asleep. I couldn't let her see.

Monday

12:43am: After Mom fell asleep, I put the statue in the oven. The orange glow dimly lit my face in the darkness of the kitchen. I sat in front of the oven door for over a half hour, watching the statue, feeling the warmth, listening for any signs of life in the house. The heat and hum from the oven lulled me into a new world governed by the ticks of the clock and the glow of the heating coils—dark corners of burning rooms—the shadow men returned. They tore at my arms and legs. They threw a shiny liquid that smelled like fish over my body, and one of the large dark figures lit me on fire. I heard my screams, saw my flesh melt from my bones. I was reduced to a blackened, sweating ribcage by the end of the ritual. But during it all, I felt nothing.

3:09am: "Eddie, I love it."

I opened my eyes.

"It's better than the picture."

My vision was a blob of white. The back of my head and body were hot. Sweat poured from my forehead. My vision cleared, and I lost breath. I rubbed my eyes but saw the same figure in front of me.

"I love it," Elizabeth said. Her hair was up in a bun. She gazed through the glass oven door. Her t-shirt was white, plain. The outline of her braless breasts was visible under the shirt. Her jeans and riding boots were dirty, caked in mud.

"I screwed up the horse. It's too big," I said to her, wiping sweat from my forehead.

"When your father first met your Mom, he whittled her a wooden rose. Took him over two weeks to get all the details just right, and it still wasn't perfect, all those petals. But it's not about perfection."

"How do you know that?"

"I don't."

She sat in front of me on the floor and peered into the oven.

"I need a father," I said.

"No you don't."

"How can you say that?" I said, wiping sweat off my forehead.

"Warm-blooded, just like your dad," she said.

"A boy needs a father, Elizabeth. I need my father." My head felt like a block of wood.

"One day, you'll know. Now clean up." She stood, knocked some mud off her boots against the cabinet, and walked toward the kitchen's entrance.

"Where are you going?" I asked.

She turned and held up my pocket-watch. It glowed in the dark of the kitchen. She was gone.

Something was definitely burning.

4:49am:

"Eddie, what the hell—?"

I stood in a frenzy. I stepped in front of Mom who had the oven door half-opened, smoke billowing out. "No, no, no, no, no! Damn it." My weekend sat in a charred pile of clay in the oven. Smoke poured out.

"What is this? Is this what you were making all this time?"

"It, I was, it was for you. I was making it for you," I said, choking on the smoke. I could only see Elizabeth's hair and part of her now blackened hand on the forehead of the crispy horse. Even destroyed, she looked beautiful.

"This was the thing you spent so much time on? What was it?"

"It was—" I thought of the first thing that came to me, "a rose." She wouldn't have been able to tell what it was. It was burned, unrecognizable to the eyes that didn't know Elizabeth's form.

Mom was still, her hands on her hips. I think she was trying to smile with her lame mouth. "Did I ever tell you that story?"

"What story?"

"I must have. Your dad—" she coughed, fanning the smoke with her hand. "He carved me a wooden rose when we were dating. When— before—" She looked as if she were trying to swallow something too big to digest. Smoke continued to exit the oven. "Get this cleaned up," she whispered, then left the kitchen.

The kitchen had a thick layer of smoke along the ceiling, but the smoke detectors didn't sound. I opened a few windows and then lifted the charred remains from the oven and placed it into the sink. My morning dose of medication waited for me, like always, only one dose. I thought of the shadow men. You. Elizabeth and what she had said to me. I placed the pills in my mouth and put my head under the kitchen faucet to get a drink of water—I wasn't ready.

I spent the rest of the morning picking the crispy layers off Elizabeth and her horse before going to school. When I removed a section of crisped clay from the top of the statue, Elizabeth's entire head cracked off. It rolled to the center of the sink and settled into the drain. Slowly, from the neck of the decapitated statue, trickles of dark red ooze seeped and spilled down the sides of her ruined body.

14.

"Eddie."

"..."

"Eddie?"

"Elizabeth?"

"It's Mom."

"Mom."

"Are you kidding?"

"What's the matter?"

"Where are you?"

"I'm just coming home from getting the food you needed."

"You never spend more than an hour at a time with me. Are you with her? Is that why you don't spend time with me?"

"It's not just because of her."

"What is it, then?"

"I need a life."

"Take me with you. You don't even make the effort to come to mass anymore. One day a week, Eddie. Would it kill you?"

"It's not just one day a week, Mom. I'm home all the time."

"Come tomorrow. Spend time with me and your grandma. She asks for you. She wants you to come play cards with her and her friends. You haven't been over her place since you were little. She won't be around forever."

"I'm busy on the weekends. I like to sleep in."

"Let's do something you want to do. I don't care. What do you want to do?"

"Nothing."

"Can we go to the stables?"

"The stables?"

"Tomorrow. It's Sunday."

"What are you talking about?"

"I'm confused."

"You said stables."

"What's wrong? It's fine if you don't want to go. Are you mad at me?"

"I just don't understand."

"Okay. Can I at least call you later? You seem annoyed. I didn't mean to—"

"Elizabeth?"

"What?"

"Is it you?"

"Who else would I be?"

"I don't know. I just thought that I was talking to someone else."

"You worry me."

"Of course I'll take you to the stables tomorrow. I'm sorry. I don't feel well."

"How many doses have you missed?"

"I'd have to count. I lost track."

"Why would you do something like that? I told you to be careful."

"You sound like my mom."

"Why would you say something like that? You don't love me."

"Of course I love you. Don't say that."

"I ask you to spend more time with me and you make excuses."

"I just told you I would take you to the stables."

"I want you to come to church with me. You're all I have."

"I feel sick."

"Tell me you love me."

"I love you, Mom."

"Just say you love me. Just tell me you love me—"

15.

"I met your mom. Now it's your turn," Elizabeth said on the phone. "Be here at six. Mom gets annoyed if people are late. She hates when people are early, too. Knock on the door right at six."

Later that night, Elizabeth and I lay on the floor in her living room, the tops of our heads touched. I threw a hacky-sack into the air and caught it each time it came back to me. There was a browned outline on the white ceiling where water had leaked. To the left of us, Elizabeth's mom sat on the couch and watched television. Her father prepared dinner in the kitchen.

"I think this is a new record," I said, focusing on the hacky-sack.

"I think you need a new hobby," Elizabeth laughed.

"What if this was my job?"

"Here we go."

"What if my job was to throw this hacky-sack into the air and catch it all day, and I made very little money. Would you still love me?"

"No." She laughed. "You could throw shit in the air all day and I would—"

"Elizabeth, that's disgusting. Watch your mouth," her mother snapped.

Elizabeth closed her eyes. I didn't care that she cursed. In fact, I liked it. It wasn't often, but when she did, it somehow made her seem more real, or made me feel more real. I went back to throwing the hacky-sack.

"Thanks. I'm glad you'd still love me if I threw shit in the air," I said.

"My mom didn't hear you say shit, but she heard me," Elizabeth said, not quietly enough.

"Elizabeth, if I hear you curse one more time, you're going to get soap in your mouth."

"Are you kidding me?" She rolled over and faced her mother.

"One more time. Try me."

Elizabeth stayed quiet. I could see that she wanted to scream the word in her mother's face, but she didn't. Elizabeth rarely talked about her mom. I could tell she knew what buttons to push. Elizabeth walked a line with her mother, always testing the boundaries, like a dog trained on an electric fence. I sadistically waited for the moment when she would tolerate the electric shock for those few moments of painful freedom.

I stopped my flawless run of hacky-sack tosses and rolled onto my side. Ever so softly, I put my mouth up to her larger earlobe and whispered, "I'm sorry." Then I kissed it.

"Elizabeth, stand up and separate yourself from him. I don't want you that close."

She never once addressed me. It was always Elizabeth's fault.

"No," Elizabeth mumbled.

"Excuse me?" her mom said, muting the television.

"You heard me. No. And, by the way, SHIT!" Elizabeth gripped the tweed carpeting underneath her.

"That's it." Her mom stood and slammed the remote control on the wooden end table so hard it broke the back and scattered plastic and batteries in every direction. She grabbed Elizabeth by the front of her shirt and pulled hard in an upward direction, almost ripping her shirt off. I heard Elizabeth's pointer nail crack in the carpet as she attempted to grip it. She shrieked. Her body jerked up and her head flew back, bouncing off the floor with a thud. Her father stopped cooking and came to the entrance of the kitchen, mouth open as if he wanted to say something, but he didn't. I sat up, but couldn't speak, not knowing if I should, if I could.

"No, no, stop it!" Elizabeth yelled.

"I told you, I will not be made a fool." Her mom clenched her jaw, held onto Elizabeth's shirt, and dragged her, as Elizabeth desperately tried to grip the rug before being pulled into the bathroom. As Elizabeth waved her hands and kicked her legs attempting to free herself, her shirt twisted even tighter around her mother's arm. Then, as Elizabeth's body writhed, her breast fell out of her bra. I hadn't seen any part of her naked body besides her neck. But this was not the way that I had wanted to see it.

"Stop it," I yelled. "It was my fault."

"Eddie, don't get involved," her father said, as if he had been where I was many times before.

Elizabeth's mom dropped her daughter onto the bathroom tiles with another thud and shut the door behind them. The click of the lock followed. Yells and cries. Slaps and gasps. I sat on the carpet, shaking. Her dad stood with his head down and leaned against the frame of the kitchen's entrance as if waiting for thunder after lightning—a slap. The cry.

My chest exploded.

I stood and hurried past her father to the bathroom door. In one steadfast motion, I kicked the bathroom door so hard my foot went partially through it, breaking the top hinge, separating the door from the wooden frame—it felt so satisfying to be unhinged, Dad. It was what I would have wanted someone to have done for me.

Elizabeth was on the floor, her eyes drowned in tears. Her mother gripped Elizabeth's shirt and held a bottle of iridescent blue liquid soap over her head. Elizabeth shielded herself with a hand and tried to push the bottle away. The back of her pastel pink shirt was torn in sections like broken wings, exposing her back. Her mom's jaw was still clenched. The blue soap was already down the sides of Elizabeth's face, on her shirt, on her bottom lip, smeared across her exposed breast, tangled in her hair. Elizabeth's eyes pleaded. Her mother stared at me, frozen.

"Leave her alone," I said.

I snatched the soap bottle from her hand, her mouth agape. I grabbed Elizabeth's shirt with one hand and her mother's hand with the other, releasing her hold. I lowered Elizabeth's body to the tile. Silence filled the space in the bathroom and bled into the kitchen.

"Take my hand," I said to Elizabeth.

She did. The whole time I helped her to her feet, she kept her eyes on mine. She adjusted her shirt and reached under it to adjust her bra. I grabbed a handful of tissues from a box on the sink behind her mom.

"Let's go," I said.

Her mom was quiet. She let us leave. We walked past her father as I said, "I'll have her back before eleven." Her dad nodded, looked at the floor, and rubbed his forehead.

It was a warm spring night. The car ride was silent. Elizabeth spent most of the ride wiping the soap from her face and hair. She cleared a patch of blood off her elbow that had been cut on the edge of the doorframe while being dragged into the bathroom. Her voice was hoarse. She attempted to say "shit" again, but it sounded more like an injured bird.

We arrived at the small parking lot of a beach. A fence lined the lake, and the gate was locked at its entrance.

"Where are we?" Elizabeth asked in a raspy voice.

"A place I go, closer than the bird sanctuary, to get away."

"Is this Lake Ronkonkoma? Isn't it closed?"

"I know a way in."

I parked the car. "Wait," I told her. I walked around the car and opened her door. "Let me help you." With one arm behind her knee and the other under her lower back, I picked her thin frame up in my arms. Normally, Elizabeth would have argued with me, not being the type to want a man treating her like some heir to a throne, but I thought this was what she needed. I carried her down the side of the fence until I came to the opening that had been cut. I walked through with her in my arms, making sure to not hit her head on the sharp metal edges.

"Is this a good place?" I asked, standing in front of a patch of sand partially littered with beer bottles and cigarette butts. We were a few feet away from the water's edge. It wasn't the fantasy I had constructed, but it was the best I could do for now, and my arms were tired from holding her.

"Sure," Elizabeth said.

I kneeled down and placed her on the beach, worried she was disappointed with the location. I removed my coat and put it over her shoulders.

"Thank you, Eddie."

"Don't thank me. I'm sorry."

"You shouldn't say you're sorry. You did nothing wrong. You saved me." She looked up at me with a face that knew the importance of the words. *Saved me,* she mouthed again. "I'm so embarrassed. I'm sorry you saw that."

"There's nothing to be embarrassed about. You think you're the only one with a fucked up mother?" Dad, forgive me. I had never confirmed it aloud to myself, to anyone before. And now, it was somehow real, and the heaviness it brought made me want to talk about anything else, even you.

"It made me so angry, watching you like that," I said, "your mom doing that to you. Is that the first time?"

"This bad, yeah. She's never gotten that crazy over something so small. Over shit."

We both laughed. Then Elizabeth quieted. So did I.

"You saw me," she said.

"What do you mean?"

"You saw me. You know—" A yellow street lamp illuminated her face, showered her in gold light. The moon was veiled by a black cloud. She looked down.

"Oh. Yeah, I think. Kind of," I said, not wanting to embarrass her anymore.

"It was only a matter of time. I mean, I've just never—well, no one's ever really seen me like that. You know?"

I didn't know if she meant that no one had ever seen a naked part of her body or that no one had ever seen her vulnerable. I didn't ask. I wanted to be the first for either. For both.

"It's strange. Our mothers—" she stopped.

"We don't have to talk about it," I whispered.

We both lay next to each other on the beach looking up into the stars. I thought of Mom, if she wondered when I'd be home. If she stared at the moon alone in the darkness of her room. I imagined what Elizabeth was thinking. The blue soap bottle. Her mother's hand twisted around her shirt, maybe her naked breast. What would have happened if I wasn't there? Who would have saved her then? Her father?—No. For every heroic act, the many desperate cries that remain unanswered, like my Silent Night with Grandma, waiting for a dead father to rescue me.

"I take medication," I said. It finally felt like the right time. Things couldn't have gotten any worse, and we were both exposed, two chrysalides clinging to a branch in a storm.

"What? For what?"

"I don't know."

"What do you mean? How long have you been taking it?"

"Since I was seven or eight."

"Is this because of your dad?"

"That's what my mom says. Apparently, I was 'off' after he died."

"How do you feel about it?"

"No one's ever asked me that," I said. "I see things, hear things that aren't there. Sometimes I sleep a lot. Sometimes I can't sleep at all. I get sick if I miss a dose. I'm usually nauseous. I always have headaches. My hands shake. I can't remember anything. I can't remember my father. I sometimes can't feel—things I should—with you. You know—"

She paused a moment and looked at a quarter filled beer bottle in the sand. "That night in the car, when we, you know? Is that a side effect?"

"Yeah."

"I didn't know."

"You couldn't." At least I had validation that the moment existed, that we actually attempted, even if it was a failed attempt.

"You think if you weren't on the medication you'd feel better or remember more? Like your dad?" she said.

"The few times I forgot to take my medicine, I remember more, but I feel worse."

She grabbed my hand. "Then stop taking them."

"I get really sick when I stop. And it's not just physical. I remember things, or I see things that—" Was I saying too much?

"I'll help you through it. Whatever happens. It can't last forever. I want to know the real Eddie. I mean, I know you're the real Eddie, but you know what I mean."

"I'd like to know the real Eddie too."

"Let's start tonight. I'll be here to help you."

"How do I do it? What do I do with the pills?"

"Hide them. Put them in a sock in your drawer. Don't let your mom know." She placed one hand on my thigh. She was cold despite the warmth of the season. "But you have to do me a favor."

"Anything," I said.

"If I ever get like my mom—"

"You won't."

"But if I—"

"You won't. You're nothing like her, and—" I stopped myself from saying it. But then I said it anyway. "And you're nothing like my mom either."

"In a couple years, we can go to school together out of state and—" she continued.

"Let's just take it a day at a time. I'm happy to be with you, here and now," I said.

We lay next to each other, staring up into the night sky. The frogs' chirps around the lake filled the void.

"What are you thinking?" she asked.

"A street near my house. Someone spray painted something in the road."

"What was it?

"It said, 'Wake up, you'll find what you're looking for.'"

"What does that mean?" she said.

"I don't know. But that's what I'm thinking of."

She looked toward me. "What are you looking for, Eddie?"

"I didn't know I was looking for something."

The clouds uncovered the moon, casting a brilliant white glow over Elizabeth. Her eyes shone.

"Maybe it's about waking up. It's in the waking up that makes the *it* worth finding. Whatever *it* is."

"I think I'm awake," she said.

"Me too."

16.

"All good things happen in the morning."

"What?"

"You heard me."

"I heard you, but I don't understand."

"Then why did you say, 'What'? You could've said, 'I don't understand'."

"If you want to get technical, yes, I could have said that. Fine. What do you mean?"

"All good things happen in the morning. The sun rises, warms our body, warms the earth: Good. We wake up, if we do, we are alive to experience, to love, to change: Good. Remember the time the doctor told us we're our tallest in the morning? Our spine is completely elongated? Especially for a five foot six guy: Good. We hope in the morning. We hope for a good day, plan, and our day is dependent upon the first hour of waking up. It sets a tone: Good. So tell me, Eddie, what's bad about the morning?"

"You just know it all, don't you?"

My ribcage—ivory, shiny, polished—sat atop some pictures across the room from me. The words came from it, but nothing moved when it spoke. I sat in a chair and waited for my bones to tell me something I didn't know.

"Take this picture, for example. This one's a bruiser, huh?"

"Which one?" I asked.

"Take a guess."

"The ice rink?"

"See, you know which one."

"It doesn't bother me. It's a great memory."

"His face is cut off."

"So?" I said. "Still a great memory."

"Let him go, Eddie."

"I can't."

"You chose to come off the medicine. To take the good with the bad. I didn't make that decision, but I have to deal with it because of your choices."

I picked up my chair and turned it around so that it was facing my bed. Somehow, I felt my ribcage staring at my back.

We sat in silence until I fell asleep in my chair.

The good with the bad

When did the pain in my chest begin? Probably before I can remember. Maybe even before my ribs had formed, an ancient ache. But the first moment I became aware of it was on the day you died. That night, Mom had burned all of your pictures in the backyard and returned to her bedroom, leaving a trail of footprints from the pit of charred photos to our house. I remained hidden behind a rose bush in the dark, watching the smoke rise from your photos, willing the steam into some sort of paternal revenant until it became the darkness. My eyes were wet and my cheeks hot. The wail of someone sobbing sounded from somewhere in the night, from somewhere inside. As I left the shelter of the rose bush to return inside, I saw it there under one of Mom's rose bushes, a fulgent fragment illuminated by the moon like star shrapnel. The one that got away. I reached under the bush and cut my wrist on a few thorns. I held it an inch from my face. It was a picture of you and me on ice skates at an ice rink. Someone took the picture too low. Your head is cut off. The top of my head just reaches your waist. Your plaid shirt is opened at the top and your blue jeans are worn at the knees. I couldn't remember the moment, but I could remember your worn jeans, the ones you wore even in summer.

"*Your dad was warm-blooded,*" Mom once told me.

"*I'd rather be warm-blooded than cold blooded,*" I said.

"*You're just like your father, Eddie.*"

I'm just like you, Dad. I'm just like you.

17.

Brightness and the smell of overturned dirt—I lifted my head from a haystack, used my hand as a visor, and surveyed the landscape. A red and brown barn stood behind me. Trees surrounded a fenced-in circular pen where Elizabeth rode her horse as it galloped in circles. The horse kicked up wet earth with each gallop.

"Eddie," she yelled. The horse slowed to a trot and approached the side of the fence near me. "Come over here."

"I'm not feeling well. I'll just watch you from here."

"How many doses have you missed?"

"I can't remember."

"You have to keep track, Eddie. You have to be careful. Make sure you drink plenty of water."

"I know. You don't have to tell me all the time." She was beginning to sound like Mom. My head felt inflated, and my eyes burned. After the fight with Elizabeth's mom, Elizabeth and I thought it best that I avoid coming back to her house for awhile. Her mom never spoke to Elizabeth about me or that night. Maybe she was embarrassed. Or still too angry. Her father suggested "letting things cool over for a bit." So Elizabeth and I began spending time elsewhere.

"I'm just trying to help you," Elizabeth said.

"How long have we been out here?"

"You've been sleeping for two days now. Is that a side effect?"

"I think. Two days—?" I began, but she was already leading her horse toward the stables to be cleaned. She and her horse danced across the surface of mud puddles. From where I was, her forearm scars shimmered in the sun with each movement like light on the undulating ocean. It nauseated me and hurt my eyes to stare at them too long, so I closed them and tried to remember Elizabeth's scars instead. But the memory that came was the day I drove her home after the movie. The day my car had a flat and she had helped me change it in the rain. That most holy bead of rainwater that hid in her chest. Though it felt as if she were already gone, more than physically, like she had left me in some other life, a parallel world to this malaise existence, and that at any moment I would awake from this side effect, cold and alone in my bed, a dose of medicine waiting on the glinting kitchen counter.

When I opened my eyes, Elizabeth and her horse quickly vanished into the barn, and what looked like the trail of a white gown followed her figure. Even her shadow was light, a blurry double like light's mirrored reflection. Her laugh faded with the wind.

He's all I have, I heard as the wind whipped. It echoed and slipped away with the breeze of the afternoon. A trail of dying gnats and flies flailed and floated inside a water-filled horse track across the mud.

Eddie.

I followed the voice toward the stables. The huff and snort of horses called from inside. Someone was sobbing. A sound I wanted to forget. I turned the corner and entered the barn. "Elizabeth? You okay?" No response. I passed horses on both sides, hanging saddles and bales of hay. "Elizabeth?" A dress with yellow polka-dots hung on the wall next to a red saddle. I knew the dress. Elizabeth wouldn't have worn that. I never saw her wear a dress, and the thought of never having seen Elizabeth in a dress made my eyes burn as if about to cry, if I could have cried at all.

A sharp metal-on-metal shrill came from farther in the stables. Another sob. I walked toward the noises, down the line of stables to the end of the barn near a storage section. The horses ceased huffing. When

I looked back, the horses were gone, the stables were empty filled only with dusty sunbeams. My chest felt filled with nails.

A squeak. The sound of rushing water. I crept to the back of the barn. The hay crunched and gave under my feet like snow—and it was snow. No more hay, just pure white, fresh powder. Yet the manure stench was stronger and slipped into my nose, sunk into my lungs. I choked, gagged, and puked thick black liquid into a mound of snow. It tasted like artificial sweetener. I wiped my mouth and approached the last stall, my legs weak. The sound of rushing water grew louder and louder until, like a rock rippling a still lake, the roof of the barn exploded. I shielded my eyes as fragments of splintered wood sprayed across the stables, revealing the shale gray sky was exposed, dropping heavy flakes of snow on me.

"Elizabeth?" I yelled.

I continued to the end of the barn near the storage corner while the wind whistled through the cracked roof remnants. And there, in the corner of the barn was a misplaced bathtub with an opaque shower curtain. Behind it, a shadow.

"Elizabeth?"

It was a woman's faint silhouette. The shadow was slender, short just like Elizabeth, not a sharp edge on her body. As I got closer, I heard the song again, that familiar song being sung softly. The voice was clear, pure, like crystal. Like sunshine.

"This house is full of ears, but I can't talk to anyone.
They've heard this one a thousand times"

Like most things, I couldn't place the song—a continual struggle to find time, words, memories.

The voice stopped. The shadow was still.

"Elizabeth?"

I walked closer, my breath fogged the curtain in front of me. I closed my eyes. My hands trembled. I grabbed the curtain and slid it aside.

When I was young, I walked in on Mom in the bathroom. She was naked, preparing for a shower. We didn't speak for the rest of the day until she said goodnight. When she tucked me into bed, she told me, "It's ok for you to see me. I'm your mother. It's only natural." *Natural.* But that was then. And I am older.

There was Mom, naked, natural, standing in the shower with heavy eyes. She extended a hand to me, the other hand on her neck. Her brown hair was longer than I remembered. It was wet and pasted to the top of her chest.

"Come in."

I knew that I didn't want to, and yet I couldn't help but to reach for her hand like a child. Her wet hands held mine and gently pulled me under the water. My right leg. Then my left.

"Mom," my voice trembled.

"Tell me you love me."

She opened her arms and put them around my body. She pulled me under the warm water as we embraced.

"Tell me you love me," she whispered in my ear. The water bounced off my face, soaked my hair. Droplets tangled in my eyelashes. I closed my eyes tightly, holding her just as tight.

"I love you, Mom," I said.

"Don't say Mom, just say you love me."

"I love—I love Elizabeth. I love you, Elizabeth," I told her.

Her head lifted off my shoulder. It *was* Elizabeth. It had always been Elizabeth. Her brown hair, her bronze skin, her larger earlobe and glittering forearm scars. We were in Mom's shower. She grabbed my hand and put it on her slippery breast. She moved it over her nipple as she closed her eyes and tilted her head back. Slowly she moved my hand down farther, then pulled me in close. I wrapped my hands around her body. I was naked too, slick with water, pressed against her. She stood on her tippy toes and wrapped a leg around me as I slipped in. She exhaled an uncontrolled breath.

"I love you, Eddie," she said to me, her nose scrunched, and she laughed. Then her freckles began to melt off her face and fall to the base of the tub with the water.

The steam rose and thickened. I could hardly see her in front of me. My chest burned hot, a heat I remembered feeling once. I could see her smile, she kissed me, and we turned in the shower as our lips met. I closed my eyes as the water hit them. And then my skin turned cold. Elizabeth's body shuddered.

"Someone flushed the toilet," I heard someone yell.

The freezing water stabbed at my face. I lost breath like jumping in the winter ocean.

"Eddie, you flushed the toilet."

"Maybe I'll catch fire."

"You're all I have."

"Who are you?"

"Your mom is on your forehead."

"You're still an idiot."

"I just want you to remember me, Eddie. I just want you—"

Familiar voice after familiar voice. I tried to hold on to them, and the kiss—she pulled away, someone pulled her away. I stretched my neck forward and reached my arms out farther, but there was nothing to hold onto. I couldn't see, but I knew my eyes were open. I sucked in to keep her lips on mine.

"There's no more hot water. The heat's gone."

The icy water stung my face. Elizabeth's lips made a popping noise as they left mine, and I was thrown upside down and onto my back.

Drops of water continued to hit my face. I rubbed my shirtsleeve over my eyes and saw a gray ceiling, a dark room. The wind whistled through an open window. Rain spattered on the carpet to my right.

"Am I dead, yet?"

My bedroom was empty. My ribcage and the photos were gone. There was still a half-moon impression in the carpet where it had sat. I almost wished my ribcage was still there. I shifted closer to the window and closed it. The toilet bowl was running and Mom was humming somewhere in the house—Silent Night.

Night descended outside, an eyes-shut-kind-of-darkness, but I only felt ready for a night-light-darkness. The streetlight near my window had burned out.

All good things happen in the morning.

Elizabeth is my morning.

18.

Early in my senior year of high school, I took off from school for another appointment with Dr. Bleakman. Mom interpreted my withdrawal symptoms as the medicine not working.

The more medicine I avoided taking, the more I started to obsess over details of images and conversations. I sat at the kitchen table thinking about what Elizabeth had said just a few nights ago at the beach, that we would get away together in a couple of years. But how would it work? I doubted that Mom would agree to let me go away to college. I would need a job, would have to save money. Maybe then we could rent a little apartment, attend a local college. I could apply for student loans. It could work.

"Mom, I need a job," I said.

"What do you need a job for?" She looked up from the novel she was reading.

"I want money."

"You don't need to work. I'll give you money." Mom had quit the florist job by then. I assumed we lived off of the money you had left us.

"I want my own money," I said.

"What for?"

I searched for a reason before blurting out, "To buy Elizabeth something. She got me a pocket-watch for our six month anniversary, and I never bought her anything. I didn't have the money." This wasn't entirely a lie. I had failed at creating the statue, and I had promised to buy her that crystal horse statue, but never did.

Methodically, Mom folded the corner of a page and set the book down. She dug her fingernails into the wood table as if someone were pulling it out from under her. "Six months is not an anniversary," she said.

"You never celebrated six months with Dad?" I leaned against the granite counter.

"We hardly celebrated anything. I'm not going to give you money for that, Eddie." She picked the book back up and continued to read, or at least pretended to.

"Why do you do that?"

"Do what?" She still stared at the page.

"Act like Dad never existed."

"I'm reading. Just take twenty dollars out of my bag." She pointed to her bag on the kitchen table. "Where is this anger coming from?"

Small wrinkles had formed around the corners of her lips, and tiny patches of hair thinned on her head, which she tried to cover by brushing her hair differently and using clips—guilt is heavy.

"I'm sorry," I said.

She put down her book again as the microwave beeped. "Can you get my tea for me?"

"One Equal and a splash of half and half?"

"I love you," she said.

I sat down at the kitchen table across from her. She grabbed the tea bag and dipped it up and down in the steaming water.

"I said I love you, Eddie."

"I love you too."

"Do you?"

"Why would you ask me that? You know I do."

"You're always with her now. And when you are home, you're in the basement, sleeping, angry. You never come to church with me and Grandma anymore."

"I'm always tired."

"I'm glad we're taking you to Dr. Bleakman today. Something isn't right with the medicine. Maybe it's the third medication he prescribed last month."

How long had it been since I had begun the withdrawal? How many doses had I missed? I would have to count all the pills I had dumped in the sock in my drawer. All the days had congealed in my head like refrigerated fat on gravy.

Mom turned on the television to avoid conflict, but instead, licks of flames and billows of smoke poured from a church. Our church. Mom raised the volume.

"...responded to a call that indicated Good Shepherd Church was on fire. We are still uncertain as to what has caused..."

Mom and I watched the story unfold. Policemen and firemen ran in chaotic lines.

"My God. Jesus Christ," Mom whispered, and she began to cry silently and recite a Hail Mary. She dropped her tea bag in the mug, splashing water over the sides. "Eddie—" She leaned forward.

"Eddie? Eddie, Eddie, Eddie—" she whispered again and again.

My cell phone rang in my pocket, so I pulled it out. Elizabeth was calling. Mom glanced at my phone, so I quickly rejected the call and changed the ringer to vibrate.

When the flames climbed to the roof of the church, I saw him. I edged my head closer to the television and squinted my eyes. There at the top of the church next to the steeple's crucifix was a man, appearing like a flickering sunspot in between the billows of smoke with his arms outstretched. The white square of his clerical collar glowed within the blackness. No matter how many times I opened and closed my eyes, the image remained.

"Our beautiful church," Mom said.

"Mom, why don't they do something. Why don't they save—" I realized that she didn't see him, that maybe no one seemed to notice the priest trapped within the inferno atop the church, but his outline was distinct behind the news reporter. Why hadn't he jumped? And then it was clear to me that he wasn't trapped. He was kneeling. He was praying.

After the fire, there was no mention of the priest, no body found in the charred remains, nothing. That night, Mom went into the backyard and swung in the darkness on the awning swing. I could hear her cries from my room like the faint jangle of chimes. I had the feeling she wasn't crying for the church, but instead that the flames ignited something else, something deeper. She left the windows open that night as if she wanted me to fall asleep to her cries. I shut my eyes so tightly to try and imagine myself on the top of that church, the heat at my back and the fall in front. Fire or fall? How hot that heat to push me over the edge. I thought of the way I would have stepped off the roof, backward, prayer position, head first. And the fall from on high, a turn in midair, eyes shut, or would I want to see the end? Would I make it to the ground, my heart failing first in the fall? But I couldn't. I couldn't picture myself dying— hitting the ground, a mid-air heart attack, the heat melting my flesh— none of it. I couldn't imagine dying. The one moment I wanted to know, the end, and I couldn't see it.

I didn't call Elizabeth back. I don't know when I called her again. I stashed my night dose in the sock with the rest of the colorful ovals. I couldn't fall asleep that night while thinking of the priest. What were his thoughts in those final moments? Why hadn't he jumped? What was his prayer? For whom did he pray? At the end of that night, though I still couldn't imagine the end of it all, one thing became clear. I'd rather burn than fall.

19.

I eventually accepted money from Mom that day, but I didn't buy Elizabeth a gift. "Don't buy things, buy experiences," Mom told me. So I bought the experience I wish I had back with you, Dad—ice skating.

Since waking up that morning, I had dry heaved already a handful of times, and my stomach had grown teeth. To make things worse, I was nervous that I had forgotten how to skate, especially when Elizabeth told me that she had never ice skated in her life. If I did remember how to skate, however, her inability was now an opportunity for me to show her how, redemption from changing the tire.

The ice rink was crowded with people when we arrived. Elizabeth held my hand so tightly that I had to let go to wipe my sweaty hand on my sweatshirt. Every few minutes, she'd look at me with the face of someone peering through a dirty window, waiting and studying my face as if I were a dormant geyser.

We sat down on a bench and began lacing our skates. To a stranger, it might have appeared like tension existed between us, but it was really absence masquerading as tension. There was nothing to say. There was nothing to feel except nausea. I only worried what Elizabeth felt, how she interpreted this absence. Finally, she said, "Are you alright? You feeling okay this morning?"

"Do I look that terrible?"

"No. Just pale. And you haven't really been talking to me."

That was the disturbing part. I thought that I had been talking to her all morning—in the car, waiting to rent skates, even right now as I thought about not talking to her—but I was talking to the Elizabeth in my head, and I forgot that version of Elizabeth was only as real as you, Dad.

"I'm just nauseous, and my stomach hurts."

"Can I do anything?"

"You can stop staring at me as if I'm going to murder you."

"I'm just worried."

"I told you this would suck."

"We didn't have to go ice skating," she said.

This annoyed me more than anything. All the effort of getting out of bed, of getting here, of enduring the strain and silence, and now it didn't seem to matter that we were here. I pretended to ignore the comment. We finished lacing our skates and walked toward the entrance of the rink.

"I need you to help me. I'm a little scared."

"Let me get on the ice first and make sure I remember," I said.

"Sure. I'll watch and learn." Maybe it was just me, but she sounded sarcastic, a tone I couldn't remember hearing from her until then. She pulled her woolen hat down over her ears and latched onto the rink's wooden perimeter.

The moment my blades cut the ice, I knew that I remembered how to skate. Even during the first lap around while staying in the middle lane, between the first-timers clutching the boards and the orange cones on the inside circle, I pumped my arms and legs, thrusting forward, the cold whip of air frosted my face, my blood burned in my thighs. The second lap was even more successful as I was comfortable enough to use the crossover technique around turns, whizzing in and out of lanes and around bodies. I was my old self. But then again, I didn't know who that was. Maybe this was a nauseated new self, but that didn't feel quite right either. No—I was a temporary self being used to find my old self, a version designed to burn after use. I skated like Quicksilver under the linked arms of a couple who glared after me. And that's when I remembered Elizabeth. I moved to the boards and looked toward the entrance of the rink, but she was gone. From behind me I felt a tug, a tug I feared was the earth pulling me toward it sooner than I had imagined. When I turned, it was Elizabeth, rosy cheeked and panting, struggling to stay upright.

"I did it!" she said. "I made it across the ice," she laughed.

"Great job. Most first-timers hold onto the boards the entire time."

"You're a great skater. I didn't think you were that good."

"I used to skate with my father before he died."

She grew quiet for a moment and looked down at the ice. Children's screams reverberated and clashed with the echo of techno music.

"What's wrong?" I said.

"I didn't know why you wanted to come. It seemed random. I'm sorry."

"Don't be. Really I only wanted to know if I could remember how to skate."

"Can you teach me to skate like you?"

"I'd rather teach you to skate like *you*."

She smiled and grabbed my hands. We stayed close to the perimeter of the rink. I held her hands tightly and skated backwards as she click-clacked her way forward. I couldn't see the direction in which I was skating, and she couldn't skate in the direction in which she could see, but we made it work. We trusted each other. At least, for awhile.

I grew distracted by watching a father and son across the ice. Each time the little boy slipped, his father pulled him up by his arm before he hit the ice. Is this how it had been? I don't remember falling. But maybe I had. Maybe it never felt like falling, or maybe I never had a reason to fear the fall because you were there. The father pulled his son's arm again, but this time the son wasn't falling. Then again. And again. Now the dad was hunched over, his face red and level with his son's. He was yelling as he pulled his son's arm again, harder, this time like the whip of a rope.

"—can't move that quickly. Eddie, did you hear me?" Elizabeth said.

"I heard you," I said. No sooner than I said the words, I was racing across the ice toward the father who was still pulling and jerking the child's arm. Bodies of skaters weaved in and out of my view, ignorant to the abuse. I lost sight of them, but they reappeared now farther away as if the rink were a frozen sea, the icy tide hauling them out toward the horizon. The father jerked the child's arm again, this time hard enough for me to believe it would snap off his body like a dried tree branch. The red-faced child's gray eyes met mine for a brief second before drowning in another throng of skaters. I pumped my legs harder, faster, feeling sick to my stomach now. Elizabeth's faint voice called something out to me, but it sunk beneath the muddled sounds of conversation and metallic music. My nausea swelled. I swallowed hard. "Let him go!" I yelled. Louder this time, "Let him go!" My eyes welled with tears, I tripped, stumbled. I didn't fall but lost all momentum and speed. Parents, the rink's referees, children, everyone had stopped skating and stood staring at my floundering—always a spectacle. Something clawed at the back of my shirt, scratched the back of my neck, a sensation I had felt once before, and it made me react without thinking. I threw my elbow around my body, connecting with something solid, but my eyes remained fixed on the spot in the crowd ahead where the father and son were. I couldn't lose them. My sight was as narrow as a child's trapped in a hallway. I pointed straight ahead and screamed as loudly as I have ever screamed in my life with a raw voice, "Let him go!" The crowd parted, provided an icy path for the direction of my pointer, but the lane opened to nothing but an empty space on the ice where the father and son had once been.

There was a bustle in the crowd, people began moving, their voices and words slowly took shape, their fingers now pointing at me, behind me, their bodies now moving past me, and when I turned, Elizabeth was face down on the ice. Skaters avoided the trail of red specks splayed starkly on the ice in a halo around her head—a sanguinary Heiligenschein.

"Elizabeth? What happened? Elizabeth, are you okay?" I scrambled to the ground next to her as she lifted herself to her knees with an upper lip of smeared gore. Her nose leaked blood as dark as Mom's roses in the night. She made an attempt to smile.

"Your elbow is made of lead," she said.

My elbow. She didn't fall and hurt herself. She fell because of me. "Elizabeth, I—I had no idea you—I wasn't thinking. There was—" I couldn't explain because there was no explanation for why I did it. I just did.

"I think I want to go home," she said.

I stood up and extended my hand out to her. She didn't take it. She stood on her own and stumbled to the rink's exit.

It wasn't the quiet car ride back to her home. It wasn't how long it took for her nose to stop bleeding. It wasn't even her hasty, metallic kiss before she left the car. It was what she said at the rink, that she wanted to go home. She didn't need me or my help. That's when I felt this wouldn't last. I didn't know it, but I sensed it—a visceral gravity. I started to believe that Mom and Grandma were right—I was dangerous.

20.

It was a humid Sunday, two days after the ice rink. The type of day that makes you feel stuck, wherever you are. A traveling carnival had setup portable rides and amusements in a nearby park. Elizabeth and I sat on opposite ends of a three person bench in front of a large inflatable fun house. The kids inside bounced, screamed, and ricocheted off the walls.

"How's your face?" I asked, still angry, not at her, but at myself. After I said it, it sounded more like I was annoyed for even having to ask.

"Better. Just a little sore now," she said without looking at me. "How do you feel?" she asked.

"I'm fine. You don't have to keep asking me, you know."

"Sorry."

"Don't say sorry. You didn't—" It didn't matter.

A mother ran after a kid who attempted to pop the fun house with a pointed stick.

"Do you want to go to the stable?" she said.

"Why do we always go to the stable?"

She shielded her eyes from the sun to look at the screaming kids. "We don't always go. And we don't have to. I just thought you liked going."

"I do. But maybe I want to do something."

"Like what?"

"I don't know. I just feel like we always do what you want to do."

"We went ice skating last time. That was your idea," she said.

"You don't have to remind me."

"I'm not saying it to remind you. If you want to do something else, just say it," she said, shifting closer to me on the bench.

I smelled onion on her breath from the bag of Funyuns she had with lunch. I turned my head to avoid the smell. My head was pounding, and my eyes stung from the burning sun.

"You can at least ask me. Do I always have to tell you I want a say in what we do?" I said.

She was quiet. A little girl yelped as she collided with a boy in the bouncy castle. A few of the parents stood around the perimeter of the house and said things like, "play nice" and "not so rough." A skywriter flew across the sky and finished the last D in *UNITED WE STAND*. Elizabeth folded her arms across her chest.

"I guess the attitude is part of the withdrawal?"

"Word of advice. That doesn't help."

"You're being mean, Eddie."

"How am I being mean?"

"Just the way you say things."

"I just said it'd be nice if you thought of me sometimes."

"I always think of you," she said.

A little girl with dirt on her cheeks grabbed the hose connecting the air compressor to the inflatable house and pulled it off.

"Forget it."

"Forget it? How can I forget it? You're telling me I don't think of you. That's bullshit," she said, tugging on her earlobe. Her profanity wasn't so cute anymore.

"Even my mom asks me what I want to do," I said.

"I'm not your mom."

"Let's drop it."

"Let's not. I know that coming off the medicine is not easy—"

"You have no idea."

"I can't imagine. I'm just trying to help you. You told me when we decided to do this, that we were doing this together. And all I've felt lately is you pushing me further away."

"I don't know what to tell you." I didn't. Since ice skating, it wasn't her bloody face, or the father and son, or her reticence on the ride home, but it was her refusal to take my hand that I obsessed over. It was my fault, and I was angry at myself. But yelling at myself didn't make me feel any better.

"And that's just it. You avoid talking about it. I've told you a few times that I can imagine getting out of here with you. Going away to college together in a few years," she said. "And I want you to come with me. But you always avoid talking about that too. You avoid talking about a future with me."

"You're only a sophomore. How the hell do you know what you want to do after high school?"

"I know what I want. I've always been this way. You know that, Eddie. I know I want to get away from here. We could go together. A fresh start. But I need to know you'll go with me."

"You can't just run away from your problems," I said.

"Who says I have problems? I'm not running, I'm starting over. With you. Honestly, what do you have here that's holding you back? What are you so scared of?"

It wasn't "what" I was scared of. It was "who." I was scared of the man I was becoming and what he was capable of while I was with her. If I ever cared for Elizabeth, I would have to let her go. She didn't need me anyway. It was what I loved about her, and yet it somehow made me feel more hollow than I already felt, like a gutted fish.

"Why do you love me anyway?" I said.

The inside of the deflating fun house was visible through the mesh windows. Six children were screaming, running around inside, scratching at the mesh, trying to find the netted exit of the now not-so-fun house. They fell and collided, scratched and clawed. Parents ran to the entrance of the house and screamed for their children to come to them. Moms pushed each other out of the way as the house began to collapse and fold inward on the kids—the deflated floor was now a polysynthetic quicksand.

"Why would you ask me that? Do you hate yourself that much?" She picked at her chipped brown nail polish. It flaked off and shimmered in the sun one last time before vanishing in the grass.

"I just don't see in me what you see."

She stopped picking her nails and turned to watch the children play. A few parents turned and stared at us. A girl, no more than four years old, ran to one of the mesh windows and screamed so loudly it made my ears ring. She gripped the mesh window with red hands. A snot bubble exploded from her nose. The child's mother ran to the window, tried to calm her and lead her to the way out. One of the carnival workers pulled kids, one by one, out of the exit. But the girl was too far gone in screams and terror.

Kids kept screaming as their parents carried them away. I saw a little boy behind the screaming girl at the mesh window. He sat cross-legged in the center of the sinking house. His body tilted sideways from the uneven dispersal of air. Calm and composed, he sat unblinking, looking directly at me, and smiled just before the inflatable house finally collapsed around him.

21.

I was sitting in my car, staring out of the driver's side window at dead leaves being swept silently by the wind into scattered lines in the street. A blue jay soared across the Stygian sky and settled on a powerline. From the blue jay's beak, a severed bird's head attached to a bloody, visceral string swung to-and-fro in the wind like a flail mace. I recalled the blue jay from the beach months ago, maybe the same blue jay, the same severed head, still picking at it, still digesting it. I couldn't for the life of me remember how I arrived here, or why I was here. Until I heard the muffled hiccup next to me. A repressed cough. The passenger seat of my car. Elizabeth, curled in fetal position, facing her door.

"Elizabeth—"

She started to cry softly, then hysterically. I knew that cry. I heard it before. But where? What had happened?

"How could you do this? What did I do? What did I do to you? I tried so hard. Please don't do this."

I know this memory. I know what comes next. The Cry. It comes to me in the form of a knocking on my ribcage.

"I'm not sure what to say," I said.

"Tell me you love me. Tell me you want to stay with me. Tell me you'll leave this place with me."

I didn't say anything. She turned her body and looked at me. Really looked at me. Her eyes bloodshot and damaged. The passenger door opened, letting in crisp air and—Mom.

"What the hell is going on? What are you doing to my son?" Mom reached out, grabbed Elizabeth's jacket, and shook her. Elizabeth shrieked.

"Get out. Get out Mom!" I leaned over Elizabeth, pushed Mom out of the car, and slammed the door. She walked back into the house and stood behind the glass front door to our house.

"Elizabeth, I just—"

"I can't believe you're doing this. I can't—I can't—" Her body heaved and jerked as she hyperventilated.

All I could say was, "I don't know what to say." I didn't. I let her leave. It happened so quickly, the end of us. Too quickly. Too quietly. The loudest quiet I've never heard.

I don't remember saying the words. Numb. She left my car and walked down the street, zippering her jacket and wiping her eyes in the opposite direction of my house. Numb. I didn't go after her. Instead, I shut my car off and walked inside the house. I thought that withdrawing from the medicine would return feeling, but I was freezing and numb. At least while on the medication, I couldn't hurt anyone but me. I finally found a way to punish myself.

As I passed Mom in the doorway, she said, "You did the right thing, Eddie."

"What have I done?"

"The right thing. It's all part of growing up."

This wasn't growing up. Growing up is for kids who want to be adults. Growing up is learning how to drive, how to apply for student loans, how to snake clogged drains. This wasn't for kids. This wasn't for teenagers. This wasn't even for adults.

When Mom retreated to her room, I sat for a moment at the kitchen table in the silence of the house. It was then that I heard it, something inside of me tearing, a sound like a ripe orange being ripped from its rind. I didn't cry, I couldn't. This was the death of something too deep for tears.

Mom entered the kitchen, holding my nightly medication in her palm and a glass of water in the other hand. There was nothing left for me to do now. I swallowed the pills and washed them down with the water. I went into my room and searched for the pills in the sock. When I opened the drawer, I turned the sock inside out. It was stained pink, blue, and yellow, but there were no pills.

It was October. My senior year of high school. Elizabeth and I missed our year anniversary by a month and a half.

22.

The following winter, it became impossible to tell the difference between dreams and reality—visits to Elizabeth's house that I might have taken, saying things that I should have said, wondering if I would have changed one word, said something differently, used a different inflection, if she'd have come back to me. Three different versions exist in my memory of one particular day. They all hurt equally in their own way. I deserve them all.

Version 1:

"Will you marry me?" I pulled out a cherry Twizzler I had bent, twisted, and tied into a ring.

Elizabeth looked at the ground, hands in her pockets, feet shuffling gravel on the top step of her stoop.

"You couldn't see yourself leaving Long Island with me, but now you're proposing with a Twizzler on my doorstep at seven o'clock at night?"

"Here. Take it. It's all I have." I got down on one knee and looked up at her.

She walked down the steps, staring at the Twizzler, like an apparition from the past here to tell me where I went wrong. "It's too late."

"Take it, Elizabeth. Take the Twizzler. It's supposed to be romantic. Give me your hand." She extended her hand, and I put it on her finger— she let me. "I love you. Do you know that? Let's go somewhere. The stable. Bet you've never been to the stable at night. How about that lake

I took you to after the night your mom—"

"I have to go. It's getting dark. And I'm getting tired of feeling this for you." She slipped the Twizzler off her finger and extended it back to me.

"Keep it. What good will it do me?" I said.

She dropped the sugary rope ring to the concrete with a click.

"Will you call me?"

"I don't know," she said.

My stomach growled. "We're going to make it. You and I are going to be okay. We'll get married. We'll leave this place together." I stood and looked into the black sky. A trail of stars fractured the sky. Then a light drizzle struck my face.

"You never were good at timing. You know that. That's why I got you—"

"—the pocket watch."

She smiled, but it was transient. When she saw me smile, her face died.

"Say you'll marry me, eventually. Say it, please. There's always enough time."

"I have to go. My mom'll be mad." She stood on her tippy toes and kissed me on the cheek. Warmth rush to my face. She turned, walked inside her house, and closed the door without looking back. I thought I heard crying when the door shut. Eyes peered out from the living room window curtains, but they weren't Elizabeth's.

"I made a terrible mistake, didn't I?" I said to the lawn gnome at the base of Elizabeth's steps.

"Yes, but you're young. It's not the end of the world," the gnome said.

Version 2:

"Will you marry me?" I got down on one knee and pulled out a cherry Twizzler I had bent, twisted, and tied into a ring.

"I hate you. I never thought I'd say it. You gave up on us," Elizabeth said.

"Just humor me and take the ring. It's all I have." I was on one knee looking up at her at the top of the steps, her arms crossed.

"You think you can break up with me, after all we've gone through, all I've gone through with you this past year, then come back and give me a Twizzler and expect me to say, 'Let's be together'? I need you Eddie—needed you." She walked down the steps with reservation, like a weight was tied to her ankle.

"Take the Twizzler. It's romantic." I tried to put it on her finger, but she grabbed it, bit a chunk off, and threw the other half into the darkness behind me.

"Let's get out of here. We can drive all night," I said.

"In two years, I'm getting out of here, but without you. It's dark. And I'm tired of this." She spit the Twizzler onto the concrete in a gory splatter like a bloody crime scene.

"Will you call me?"

"No," she said.

"We're going to make it. You even said so yourself, on the pocket-watch. There is always enough time." I rose and looked into the starless sky. It didn't rain.

"You suck at timing. I don't know why I got you that pocket-watch. It never did you any good. I'm going in. My mom's waiting."

She turned to leave. I grabbed her hand, but she responded with a quick elbow to the center of my chest. I lost breath, stumbled back and gasped. She walked inside her house and slammed the door without looking back. I thought I heard laughing.

"I made a terrible mistake, didn't I?" I said to the lawn gnome at the base of Elizabeth's steps.

"*You're an idiot,*" the gnome said.

Version 3:

"Will you marry me?" I got down on one knee and pulled out the crystal horse figurine she'd wanted. It was all I could afford.

She looked down at me from the top step of her stoop. "Really? You mean it? You want to be with me?" she asked.

"I always have." I was on my knee looking up at her.

Her face blushed. Tears shimmered in her eyes. "There's always enough time," she said.

"Isn't it romantic? Is it all how you'd imagined it?" I placed the crystal horse in her palm—she let me. "I love you. Do you know that? Let's get out of here. Let's go somewhere and celebrate."

"I can't tell my mother. We'd better hurry. It's getting dark. I want to leave before the sun sets."

"Why?"

"It scares me. I want to leave in daylight."

"We're going to make it. We'll go to college together, get married. It's going to work this time." A Twizzler-red sun was beginning to set.

"We'd better hurry before it's too late," she said.

"There's always enough time."

"Let me go inside and grab my things."

She stood on her tippy toes and kissed me on the corner of my lips. My face warmed. She turned and walked inside her house, glancing back at me with a scrunched nose and smile before closing the door.

I rubbed my sore chest and waited in front of her house for three years. She never came out.

"What happened this time?" I asked the lawn gnome at the base of Elizabeth's steps.

With a smile on his face, the gnome said, *"You're still an idiot."*

23.

Mom's screams woke me early one morning. I jumped out of bed and ran into her room. Nothing. Another scream. I ran into the kitchen. The grandfather clock ticked. The ceiling creaked. A third scream came through the open kitchen window. I rushed to the pane. Mom was in her white nightgown on her knees in her rose garden, drowning in colorful petals. She clutched a handful of flowers to her chest. I hurried downstairs and into the backyard.

"My God. Why would someone do this?"

I placed my hands on her bony shoulders. "What happened, Mom?"

"Someone cut them," she cried. "Who would do this? My father's roses." The roses were scattered across the ground, each rose cut clean from the stem close to the bud.

I kneeled next to her in the grass. "They'll grow back."

"That's not the point! Someone cut them."

The April sun was already strong, bleaching everything in warm light. "It's Liz. She did this."

"Mom, she would never do this. It's been months." At least, the Elizabeth I thought I knew wouldn't have.

"She resents me. This has never happened. You break up with her and all my roses get cut." She raised a handful of petals to her face and inhaled. I helped her collect the roses and put them in a giant aluminum bin she used for her tools. Mom filled it with water instead. To her, the flowers were still alive, still worth saving even when severed from its origin.

"You don't still talk to her, do you Eddie?" she said, closing the top of the bin. She grabbed my hand. "If you ever talk to her again, it'll break my heart."

"I don't, Mom."

"Promise me you won't."

"I won't. I promise."

That night, I took my medication and left the house after Mom fell asleep. I drove around Elizabeth's neighborhood. I passed her dark house. Her empty driveway. Then I drove to where I had heard she started a new job, a hardware store in Holbrook, the next town over. I walked through the automatic doors and paused, spotting Elizabeth putting green bottles of mosquito repellant away on one of the lower shelves near discounted garden shovels. It was hard to catch my breath as a gust of hot air smacked me in the face. She didn't say anything to me, but no matter—I could hear her voice in my head whispering *hello*.

A tall boy at the center of the store was mixing paint for the only other visible customer.

"Excuse me, sir, but where do you keep the, the—" I had forgotten that I had no purpose for entering the store in the first place except to see Elizabeth. I spit out an uneasy, "twine?"

"You sure that's what you want?" he asked.

"Yes."

He led the way, over a few aisles, to a giant wall of twine. I thanked him.

"Don't mention it. Good luck up there."

Twine? Twine? I was a train wreck. Dr. Bleakman changed one of my medicines, increased the dosage. Insomnia had clenched its infectious teeth in me. I had sat in Bleakman's waiting room just a few weeks prior, alone, going to the doctor appointments without Mom now, old enough to blindly follow. There were three other people in the waiting room with me. A song played on the stereo.

Something pure to burn away the darkness
that hides inside my mi—mi—mom—mom—mom—

The CD skipped on the word "mind," which made it sound like "mom," turning the melancholic melody into a bad dream. There were no receptionists in sight. Then the skipping sped up.

mom—mom—mom—mom

There was a mother and her child and an old man sitting with me in the room. They didn't seem affected by the skipping. The old man read his magazine and the mother and son stared at the wall across from their seat. The song got louder.

mom—mom—mom—mom

I held my hands to my ears, expecting them to bleed at any moment. They called my name and the song stopped. I mentioned the skipping song to the receptionist, but she returned the comment with a raised eyebrow.

Life was a small waiting room. I spent countless hours in a waiting room. Waiting for relief for one side effect or another. I was waiting, and waiting, and waiting. Every day waiting. I sat in rooms with strange people, with psychotics, derelicts, and even more frightening, normal people. But every day, another waiting room, and still no relief—she never came back.

And here I was, thinking of a waiting room in front of a giant wall of twine, different brands, colors, thicknesses, and lengths. For the next few minutes, I stood in awe, half-wondering why there were so many colors and half-wondering why a hardware store was open so late. I pulled out my wallet and found my last five dollars. I reached into my other pocket and located a crumpled piece of paper I had been carrying around with me since we had broken up. A piece of paper that had dialogue lines, pre-written conversations I thought we might have had if the opportunity arose. I didn't want to risk sounding like an idiot if a situation presented itself, especially because I didn't know if I would only have one chance to make it all alright. I grabbed the brightest roll on the wall—a luminous neon orange. Maybe then she would notice me. As I turned to walk out of the aisle, I saw the reflection of someone in the frame of the chrome shelving. At first, I thought someone was directly behind me. But no. It was my own pale, gaunt self staring back like a blanched, gutted jack-o-lantern left out long after the season had ended.

A lady about Mom's age stood next to Elizabeth at the counter. Her name tag read: *Rose*. I handed Rose the twine. She looked at me funny and then let a smile escape as if she knew everything that had happened over the past few years.

I fidgeted with the five singles in my pocket as the lady waited and smirked. What if I don't have enough money? Why do I only have five dollars? Why am I sweating so much? Why am I here? And then, Elizabeth turned around from nervously organizing things on the counter. Her hair was in a ponytail and her work shirt half untucked. I can't remember her looking at me once, but I can remember her tugging on her larger earlobe.

Before I knew it, Rose handed me my change. The interaction was so quick that I didn't even remember giving her the money. I crumpled the receipt and my change into one bunched mess and stuffed it into my pants pocket while still looking at Elizabeth, her looking down at the counter. The lines—I forgot about the paper with the lines of dialogue. I had to act before I was once again too late. This was my chance. I unfolded the piece of paper, but the only thing on it was *Hey.*

"Hey, Elizabeth."

"Hi," I think she whispered.

"Someone cut all of my mom's roses last night."

"I'm sorry to hear that." She wasn't looking at me, but instead at the counter, and pretended to refill or fix a stapler.

"I miss you."

She didn't respond. She just cried and ran into the back of the store. The paint mixer came to the front of the aisle with his hands on his hips.

"You're an idiot," Rose said.

"So I've been told," I said.

I took one more look at the stapler and then left the store. I tried to catch my breath walking back to the car. I looked at the twine in my hand and then put it in my breast pocket. My car was in the parking lot under a tree I hadn't noticed when I parked. Its sharp branches stabbed at the dark. No foliage. No flowers. Just bare, sharp branches that made me feel nauseated and naked. I drove out of the parking lot and headed home. I walked directly into the backyard and grabbed an armful of roses from the bucket. One by one, I tied twelve roses with the twine back onto the stems. Sharp thorns pricked me, and blood ran black down my wrists in the night. I went inside, rinsed off, and fell into a superficial sleep with throbbing fingers and an aching head. I awoke often in hot sweats after nightmares of falling into thorny trees with no one to pull me out. Sometimes I still awake in the dark, searching for words, reaching out for something on an invisible shelf.

24.

I tried to live a normal life without Elizabeth. I stopped going to her job. I stopped trying to see her. I stopped everything. A normal life? No—a normal life would have been a life with her in it. I tried to live an abnormal life. Actually, that's not entirely correct either. A normal life wouldn't be with her, it would be with you, a boy and his father. An ideal existence would be a life with you *and* her. So really, there's only an abnormal life and a perfect life. So I tried to live a miserable life without both of you. I can imagine it's probably like someone being born with perfect vision, then being stricken with blindness. I'm not sure whether it's better to have never seen at all or to be tortured with the imaginings of a once was.

I was twenty years old, still living with Mom, attending my first year at a local community college, before I dropped out. I noticed a girl sitting across the coffee house with a laptop, leaning against a large window. A snowstorm brewed outside. She looked like Elizabeth. She had her brown hair and bronze complexion. Some freckles, even. No larger earlobe, of course, and not as short. But close. Was it Elizabeth? No, it wasn't. That would have been something.

"Excuse me, but you're staring at me. Is something wrong?" Her eyes were burning holes through my face. She was now standing directly in front of me.

"I wasn't staring," I lied.

"No, I'm quite certain. I'm usually right about these things. Ninety-nine percent sure, in fact."

"How can you be certain this isn't the one percent case?"

The skin between her eyebrows twitched and her mouth hung open.

"Don't get all shy on me now," I said. "You came all the way over here to accuse me of staring at you." A bit strong for not knowing her. What did I have to lose? I lost Elizabeth. Lost a father. I had plenty of medication: a recipe for instant happiness. I thought she'd slap me. Maybe I wanted to feel the sting of my own mortality.

"I have perfect eyesight." She sat down in front of me now and talked faster than before. "And I specifically saw you staring at me."

"Are you one-hundred percent sure your eyesight is perfect, or are you only ninety-nine percent sure?"

For a few moments, there was silence. Then we both laughed in disbelief at the absurdity of it all. I couldn't remember the last time I had laughed.

"I'm Elizabeth."

I lost breath. "What? What did you say your name was?"

"Lisa."

I exhaled. "Eddie." We shook hands. "You look like someone—" I stopped myself, not because I didn't want to ruin our relationship this early, but because I didn't want to disgrace Elizabeth by comparing her to anyone. There's only one Elizabeth. All others are carbon copies—unconscious projections.

"I should hope we all look like someone," she said.

I only smiled out of politeness. I had heard that one before. "Sorry for staring."

"So you were?"

"I thought you were someone else."

"Come on. How cheesy is that."

An awkward silence.

"What now?" I said.

"You ask me out for a drink, dinner, whatever."

"Do you want to go out for a drink, dinner, whatever?" I said.

"The whatever sounds great. I remember having that as a kid. My mom used to make—"

"Alright, alright, I get it. You win."

"I love winning."

Her head turned down, but her eyes looked up at me. She smirked with eyebrows raised. This was something I had never seen in a woman, not in my mother or Elizabeth. This was confidence, and I suddenly felt uncomfortable. Then my discomfort made me feel something akin to embarrassment, like how I felt after Elizabeth changed my tire in the rain. Like I should be in control, have all the answers, like I should be the one with confidence. Instead, Lisa's confidence made me feel like a dandelion seed in a gust of wind.

"How about dinner Saturday?" she asked.

"Okay," I said.

She stood, walked back to her table, jotted something down on paper, put her computer and papers away, and left a note next to me before she walked out the door. I guessed at what the note said before looking at it:

Eddie, Loved our conversation, but I'm not Elizabeth, so we won't last. -Lisa.

P.S. Here's my number if you want to carry this on longer than it has to: 354-922-3848.

From the day I met Lisa to the day we went out, I thought about what it meant to go out on a date with her. My days were filled with guilt from having spoken to Lisa the way I had and for asking her to go out to dinner. Technically, she asked me to ask her, but I still repeated what she told me to say. Elizabeth might understand why I did what I did. But then there was the guilt of getting involved in another relationship because I had a responsibility to Mom—to you. It was one of the reasons why I had ended my relationship with Elizabeth. This was not a promising beginning.

Saturday took it's time arriving. Saturday wanted to let the thought of Lisa eat at my guts. More than once, I attempted to pick up the phone to call it off and tell her I was sick, busy, dying. More than once, I sat in my car outside Elizabeth's job between Wednesday and Saturday wanting to tell her. A couple of times, I puked. Finally, I called Lisa and stuttered, "When and where?" I spent the last hour before our date dry heaving into the toilet.

It was a small Italian restaurant, Momma Lombardi's—Elizabeth's favorite place. I, of course, was late by about ten minutes, despite it being blocks from my house. To be honest, I don't know why I was always late. Gaps of my day seemed to vanish without me knowing until they were gone.

The restaurant reminded me of a Mediterranean painting I'd seen on the Home and Garden Channel: dim lighting, mahogany tables and chairs, crown molding with cherubs holding harps. A portly, dark haired gentleman escorted me to a table located in the back near a window. It overlooked a snow covered parking lot where a group of dark skinned men gathered for a cigarette after bringing garbage to the dumpster.

"I will escort Ms. Lisa to the table when she arrives."

"Are you sure she's not here yet? I'm late. I was supposed to meet her at 7:30."

"I'm sorry, but your date has not yet arrived."

Date. The word made me nauseous. I don't date. Dating meant I was going through a phase of being without Elizabeth. Everybody and everything was relative to her. Do I sound obsessive, Dad? I was. I am. I always have been.

The room hummed with the conversations of suited men and shiny women. Was I underdressed in my khakis and polo? Maybe if I had a father, I would have known how to dress for certain occasions, or I would have at least had someone to tell me not to worry about what others think. An old piano player keyed a tune that frequently changed tempos. His body swayed with the music, and his eyes were closed for most of the song. He hummed something loud enough for the crowd to hear him over the piano. I hated old people.

I took out my pocket-watch: 7:50. As I waited, I traced its beveled inscription with my pointer: *To my love, There is always enough time.* She was twenty minutes late. I was always the late one. Normally, this would be the part of the date where the date would start sweating and questioning whether or not he would be stood up. But the thought of Lisa not showing actually eased some of my anxiety. Maybe she'd gotten cold feet. If she didn't show, I'd still have had the chance to eat a dinner alone prepared by someone other than Mom. As soon as I began to feel relief, Lisa crossed the threshold of the room. The voices in the restaurant quieted, and the piano player changed his tune to a soft nocturne, Chopin, I think. And Lisa looked like—

Sometimes there are moments we stop. Even me. Acknowledge something for what it is. This was one of those moments. When you recognize something without filters, without bitterness or judgment. Lisa was beauty.

My lungs expanded and held their position. I didn't forget about Elizabeth, I just recognized Lisa. There was a perfect balance of skin and material, a proportionate level of grace and confidence in her walk to the table. Her appearance shaded myth and reality. Her shiny black dress glittered like the moonlight on the sea. Her henna hair bounced with each step, seemingly weightless. This was the closest I had come to seeing Elizabeth in a dress, a mere representation.

"You showed." She smiled.

"Why wouldn't I?"

"You sounded like a wreck on the phone. Did you puke?"

"A few times. But at least I was on time." I kept my lateness a secret.

"Yes, you win."

"I also like winning."

She smiled. I rose and moved toward her to help with her chair.

"Thank you, Ed."

I've always hated being called Ed. She didn't know that. Elizabeth did. I didn't have the heart to tell Lisa. She probably thought it was cute. As I pulled out her chair, I looked down the V of her dress as she shifted up to the table. I immediately felt embarrassed.

There we were, across from each other, two strangers in a restaurant without even the slightest idea as to what we had in common. It sounded like the beginning of a cheesy romance movie. But this wasn't a movie. This was my life.

She grabbed her menu and began perusing the list. "Have you been here before?" she said.

If she only knew I had been here with Elizabeth a few times. "I heard it's pretty good," I said.

"It looks fancy."

I took some time looking at the menu, but already knew what I would order. Ravioli marinara, not baked, the way Elizabeth and I liked it. We'd agreed it was too much cheese in one meal.

"You know what you want?" she asked.

"Ravioli Marinara."

"I'm getting the baked gnocchi," she said using an Italian accent. She stopped looking at her menu and placed it down, keeping her eyes on me. "What's wrong?"

"What?"

"I'm good at sensing when someone is off, or upset. You seem distracted."

"Why do you say that?"

"You haven't looked at me once since you sat down, with the exception of looking down my dress."

Dammit.

"Are you nervous? Or maybe it's not nerves. You just said 'Why do you ask' instead of 'No' right away, which means there is something wrong. So now I think something's wrong."

I was distracted. And it was exhausting comparing Lisa to Elizabeth. How do you tell a date you're thinking about another woman? "You want to know the truth?"

"Uh-oh. What is it? You're worrying me, and we haven't even ordered our food."

"I haven't been myself since my last relationship. That's all."

"Who have you been?"

"I wish I knew." *I wish I knew if I was anyone at all, even someone else.*

"I understand."

"It's not you, trust me. Wait, that sounds terrible. I should say there's nothing wrong with you. Or there's something wrong with me. This isn't going well."

She laughed. "Of course it is. Don't be so serious. Don't be so intense. We're just eating food. I'm just a girl you stared at in a café, and now you're making it up to me by taking me out to dinner. That's all."

I couldn't deny it. I already enjoyed being around her. She made me laugh, something no other woman had been able to do except Elizabeth. It felt good to laugh. The last authentic act of emotion I was still able to express.

"Thanks."

"Don't thank me."

The waiter came to the side of our table. "Good evening. Are you ready to order?" he asked.

"I'll have the baked gnocchi."

"And I'll—"

"He'll have the ravioli. Not baked. Marinara." She looked over at me and smiled again. She loved smiling, and I didn't mind her smile either. But when she ordered for me, I felt that familiar visceral discomfort return. I even looked around at the other diners to see if they had heard her order for me.

"Is that it?" the waiter said.

"Yeah. That's all, thanks."

The waiter gathered our menus and walked away.

"He didn't ask us for drinks," she said.

"We look like children."

"We are children," she said.

"Then why are you surprised?" I said.

"I don't know. Why aren't you?"

The tension between us contracted and expanded like a rubber band I never wanted to snap.

"So who are you?" she asked. "I don't know anything about you except that you go to that café."

"True. How about this," I began. "If we were married for a few months, and I was involved in a horrible car accident and lost my arms and legs, would you stay with me?"

"What kind of first date question is that?" she said.

"The only important question to ask."

There was still a constant hum of conversations in the room. The piano player was taking a break, talking to an old woman by the bar, laughing and occasionally putting his hand on her shoulder as if he had known her all his life. The waiter came to the table again.

"I'm sorry, but would you like something to drink?"

We smiled at each other. I grabbed the wine list and picked out the first thing my finger found.

"We'll have a bottle of 2007 Dr. Loosen Riesling."

"Fine, Fine. Anything else?"

"That'll be all."

The waiter left the table.

"Smooth. I can't believe he didn't card us," she whispered.

"So how old are you?" I asked.

"Twenty," she said. "You?"

"Me too."

"How old was your ex, if you don't mind me asking."

It hurt to hear 'ex' used in reference to Elizabeth, like remembering you have a broken leg after putting pressure on it again. "When I first met her, she was fifteen."

"And how old were you?"

"Seventeen."

"Those young girls are trouble."

"No they aren't," I snapped. Elizabeth was the good one. I was the fucked up one. It made no difference. She didn't have to know. I didn't want to talk about Elizabeth to Lisa. I shouldn't have even used their names in the same sentence.

Lisa looked down at her napkin and began to fold it over and over again.

"I'm sorry," I said.

"Don't be."

"Anyway, you never answered the question," I said.

She looked up and smiled. "I thought you'd forgotten."

"I never forget."

"Yes."

"Yes what?"

"Yes, I'd stay with you."

"What if we were just dating?"

"Yes."

"No you wouldn't," I said.

"What?"

"You wouldn't stay with me if I lost my limbs and we were just dating. Only if we were married and only because it's marriage."

"Why do you ask me questions if you're just going to answer them for me? Don't ask me if you aren't going to believe me," she said.

"I'm sorry. You're right."

"Marriage doesn't mean anything to me. I mean, it does, but if we're in love, I'd stay with you whether you lost your legs, your arms—or your dick." A few people turned and glared.

"One decibel too loud," I said with a smile. It reminded me of the time Elizabeth yelled 'shit' at her mom, and it suddenly made my stomach ache as if I hadn't eaten in days.

"Sorry about that," she said.

"Don't be. I needed this. I haven't been out—"

"Ever? It doesn't show."

We leaned into each other and laughed in whispers until the waiter came back with the wine wrapped in a nice white towel and a pair of long stem wine glasses between his fingers.

"Your wine." He placed the glasses down on the table and handed me the bottle.

He raised his hand as if I should take a sip. So I did. I tipped the bottle back and began drinking.

"Whoa, whoa, whoa! No, no, no!" The waiter quickly took the bottle from my hands. Couples around the room stared and scoffed, some laughed. Lisa cupped her mouth, trying to stop herself from laughing.

The waiter poured the wine into the glasses, swirled it, and offered me a sip. I drank and smiled at the waiter.

"The food will be out shortly."

The pianist returned to his piano. There was a microphone set up next to his piano.

"I ah, will be taking some ah requests." He improvised softly on the piano under his speech. "So ah come on up and ah let me know if you'd like to hear somethin' nice. Come up and dance. En—ah—joy your night."

"That's nice," I said, looking back at her.

"What is?"

"I wish I were born in the forties. When kids our age appreciated that kind of stuff."

"I know what you mean." She was quiet a moment. "What was she like?"

"Who?"

"Your ex."

"You jump around a lot in conversations."

"She must have been something really special."

"Why do you want to know about her?"

"'Cause I like you. And I want to know what makes you tick."

This was an understatement. Elizabeth was my pacemaker.

"I don't know. She was just, different."

"How?"

"She was honest. She didn't let anyone change her, even me. She didn't have a mean bone in her body. She tried to—love me for who I was. What I am."

"Who, or what, are you?"

"I don't know."

The piano player sang and played.

> *"I can't stop loving you*
> *I've made up my mind*
> *To live in memory*
> *Of the lonesome times"*

"I love this song," she said, looking deep into the restaurant. "Do you want to dance?"

"Dance? Here?"

"Yeah, come on. Let's get up and dance over there." She motioned with her head to an open spot in front of the piano. "The piano player said we could."

"I'm not really a dancer."

"Please. Dance with me. I haven't danced with a guy since my dad danced with me at my sweet sixteen. And he's dead. So it's an emotional sore spot for me, and you wouldn't want to bring up painful memories and make me cry spontaneously in the middle of this romantic Italian restaurant on our first date, would you?"

Could there have been something meaningful to this? To us? Or just a bond of loss? Before I knew it, she grabbed my hand and pulled me up to the dance floor near the piano. Everyone watched as we passed them in their seats. The music swelled as we approached. We stopped in the clearing on the floor. She turned and faced me. She was my height in heels. Grabbing my hand, she pulled her body close to mine. Her breath smelled like winter.

"You're going to lead, right?" she said.

"Do I have a choice?" I had never really slow danced before, except one time with a girl in elementary school to "Farmer in the Dell." And we only really hugged and waddled. I never had the opportunity to dance with Elizabeth. Our chance just never came.

"I can't stop wanting you
It's useless to say
So I'll just live my life
In dreams of yesterday"

"You're a pretty good leader," she said.

"Thanks. I don't always get the chance," I said. "You're a pretty good follower."

"To be honest, following is not my strong suit."

"Those happy hours, that we once knew
Tho' long ago, still make me blue
They say that time, heals a broken heart
But time has stood still, since we've been apart"

Maybe it was the music, or the lighting, or the cherub crown molding, but here, I was someone else, someone who knew his father was proud of him, someone who Elizabeth wanted to be with, a man who didn't make mistakes, a man who was always on time, who didn't feel obligated to his mother, who wasn't on pills. I tried to hold back tears, but one escaped from my right eye. It felt good, the sting of sadness. We were dancing so close. She brought her face to mine—blue eyes I hadn't noticed until she was directly in front of me. My tear was running down my cheek, behind schedule, and that's when she kissed me, but not me, the tear, before it fell off my cheek, slowly, taking her time, consuming every ounce of the salty drop.

"I love you, Elizabeth," I whispered.

"I love you, too," she said.

We danced the rest of the song, and a few songs after. I lost track. All I know is that she kept her head on my shoulder the whole time. Our plates steamed on the table across the room. At the end of the final song, she took her head off my shoulder and led the way back to our table as a few couples clapped. We didn't do anything spectacular as far as our dancing was concerned, but they seemed to like whatever it was that they saw.

"Ed, I like you."

"Lisa I—"

"Can't we just leave it at that?"

"I wish we could."

"Then let's at least finish our dinner, joke a little more, and take it slow, okay? Can we do that?"

"Sure."

We ate dinner, talked about our lives, our families. I didn't really tell her anything about my parents except that you had passed away when I was young, and that I lived with Mom. She had a sister away at college. Her father had died in 9-11, a fire chief who entered and never exited. We laughed at some of the old couples around the room, their formality and senility. Then we reached the bottom of our plates and the last sip of wine.

"I had a really nice time with you, Ed."

"I don't like Ed."

"I'm sorry. I think I've been calling you Ed this whole time, thinking it was cute."

"I didn't have the heart to tell you."

"I hope you have the heart to tell me anything at this point. I mean, you practically stalked me."

We laughed, then there was silence.

"Is this the last time I'm going to see you, Eddie?"

"Do you want the truth?"

"Is it that bad?"

To tell you the truth, Dad, I didn't know the answer to her question. I had no idea whether we would see each other again. I was in love and had always been in love with Elizabeth. What was the point of dragging this out, of hurting another girl?

"I don't know, to be honest."

"Don't know what? Don't know if you want to see me again?"

"Yes."

"Ouch. Is it her?"

"Yeah."

"How about giving me a few more chances. Give me some time to show you we can have a good time together."

I didn't deserve her company. That much, I knew. "I did have a good time, Lisa. That's the problem."

"Can I show you more good times? Wait, sorry, I sound like a hooker."

"I don't want to hurt you."

"I can take it. I'm a big girl."

I knew she'd get hurt. I just prayed I wouldn't hurt her in my car again.

25.

For some time after, Lisa continued to make me laugh. Every time I saw her, she had some way, some charm to keep me around for one more night. As she finished applying eye makeup in the mirror, I stood in the entrance of her apartment, a tiny off-campus loft a block from Stony Brook University where she studied.

"Why are we going to this concert if you aren't in the band anymore? Not that I'm complaining," she said.

"I saw Mr. Nostaga at Stop and Shop. He told me to stop by and see the new group of jazz band students. Some of the old players are going to be coming back to play with them tonight."

"How come you're not playing with them?"

"I haven't played in years."

"So you're kind of a retired celebrity?"

"Washed up is more like it. Let's get going. I don't want to be late."

We left her apartment and walked into the night. The cold air tasted metallic. On the drive to the concert, Lisa asked me something that she'd asked me many times before.

"How do you feel about us?"

"I like you a lot, Lisa."

"Like—that all it's ever going to be?"

"I told you in the beginning that—"

"I know. I'm not blaming you." Her voice trembled on 'you.'

"I'm still here with you. You've kept me here this long."

"I don't want to just keep you here. I want you to want to be here. Why should I have to keep you here?"

Our relationship was a reticent understanding expressed through eyes and absent words. We never made our relationship official, as many young relationships do. I didn't want to make it official because it didn't ever quite feel official.

"Can you roll up the window? I'm cold," Lisa said.

We remained silent for the rest of the car ride. The moon slipped behind some thin clouds, outlining them with its nickeled glow. The sky looked like a paper towel commercial, when they'd put a pound of grapes on a sheet and the bottom would bulge and droop to test its strength. I ground my teeth and pulled the key from the ignition in the school parking lot. Lisa appeared brittle in the passenger seat of my car, her hand up to her mouth while looking out the window and chewing on her fingernails.

"We're here." I leaned over and gave her a kiss on the cheek. She gave me a half smile that reminded me of Mom's lame smile.

We walked into the school holding hands. Her hand wasn't clammy or cold. It was warm and soft. Could it get better? Could the thought of Elizabeth and my guilt for neglecting Mom wane over time? I wanted to kiss Lisa, to reassure her that things would work out. It was wrong of me, Dad, for bringing her that far in a state of *What are we?* I would have to talk to her that night. I would tell her that I wanted to make it official. I wanted for her to be in an official relationship with someone who thought of her as I did about Elizabeth. Maybe I could eventually think of Lisa in that way.

The auditorium was buzzing with parents and students as we settled into our seats. Mr. Nostaga, now a more hunched and bald man with glasses, stood center stage in front of maroon curtains.

"Thank you all for coming." His eyes fell on me. "Especially some of my former students. Let's hope we can finish this concert before the snow comes. I'll try to talk less than the last concert and get you home at a reasonable hour. I'm very proud of the work these kids have accomplished and the effort they've made over the last few months. You'll notice some old faces in the band for the opening number. I asked alumni to play the first song with us. Our first number is Ray Charles' 'I Can't Stop Loving You.' Enjoy."

"Do you remember that song?" Lisa asked, elbowing me in the center of my chest, and only then did I notice that this spot on my chest was sore, but I couldn't remember being injured there.

The curtain opened, revealing about thirty high school students with gold and silver instruments shining under the auditorium lights. I recognized a few people as I scanned the young faces. I remembered that feeling, the tension in the moment prior to playing the first note of the first song, the anticipation unbearable. The silence before the first note was my favorite moment of the entire performance. Like a bomb plummeting to earth, eyes skyward, time stops, and the only sounds are the quiet breaths and the closing of eyes bracing for impact.

I waited for this moment gripping the armrests of my chair. Mr. Nostaga raised his hands, and as he raised them, the spot that was once covered by his forearm was revealed—it couldn't be. I blinked a few times and sat forward in my chair. It couldn't be. An hallucination? Another side effect of the medication? A face that blurred all things around it, as it did when I first saw it long ago in the band room. Her lips pursed around the mouthpiece of the saxophone. Her unadorned fingers caressed the instrument's keys. Her bronzed skin seemed to blossom under the spotlights like something raw burgeoning from the earth. Her right hand quickly tugged on her larger earlobe, but I imagined no one else noticed. I should have known she'd be there. Or maybe I knew all along—the reason I came.

My heart beat louder than the crowd's rustling of programs. I inhaled, and then Nostaga's hands came gently down with the first note. It became a habit of mine to always shut my eyes when the first note was played in any performance. Before that night, keeping my eyes open for the first note of the performance was like keeping my eyes open while sneezing—impossible. But this night, watching Elizabeth, I kept my eyes open. The song wrapped around me, almost smothered me. The band crescendoed and goose bumps covered my arms, neck, and scalp—touched by the hand of God, immobile, mute, breathless.

When it was over, I think the audience clapped. I couldn't move my eyes from her. She vanished. Her song was finished, and she was gone as quickly as my time with you.

"Eddie? Eddie? Why aren't you clapping?" Lisa nudged me in the ribs with her elbow. I touched earth and moved my arms in and out in some sort of clapping motion.

"I can—am. I am."

"What?" she asked.

"I'm clapping," I mumbled. I couldn't take my eyes off her empty chair, glowing under the spotlights, for the rest of the performance, like a lost traveler mistaking a distant will-o'-the-wisp for a beacon of light.

I debated leaving, excusing myself to go to the bathroom, but really to search backstage, to see her one last time. I glanced over at Lisa. She was smiling. She was happy. She was beautiful. She wasn't Elizabeth. It was my punishment for ruining the real thing. I wanted to say something sweet, something that would keep her around without keeping her forever. To keep her just enough time until Elizabeth came back to me—but how cruel. Who had I become? I knew what I had to do just as I had known with Elizabeth. But until then, I sat in my seat for the rest of the concert, sweating, imagining, hoping, furtively scanning, and slouching in my chair. I waited for most of the people to leave the auditorium. I didn't want Elizabeth to see me with another girl. While walking out, Lisa asked me twice what we were waiting for. I stayed quiet, but alert, making sure Elizabeth had left.

"You're acting strange" Lisa said.

"I'm just tired."

"What did you think? Are you happy you went?"

"I felt young again."

We made small talk all the way out to the parking lot. Large snowflakes descended from the black sky as we sat in the car, allowing the engine to warm and the heat to seep. Lisa stared out the window into the snow.

"Thanks for coming," I said.

"No problem." She was looking at me now. "It was a nice concert." She shifted in her seat as if unable to find a comfortable position. I put the car into drive and left the lot.

The snow was falling heavier than before. I was no longer looking at the road. Instead, I let my eyes focus on the giant flakes glimmering in the headlights for the last time, flickering before crashing into the windshield, plummeting into lakes, atop rusty mailboxes and shirts left out from the summer. Each flake falling from some high invisible ledge. My mouth salivated as it typically did before throwing up, but I didn't feel nauseated. I wondered what Elizabeth might be thinking. Or if she'd remember that day at the Hallmark store in the blizzard—when we kissed. I could taste her mint chocolate tongue.

"Lisa," I said. "I'm not in love with you."

"I know."

She cried. You can tell a lot about people by the way they cry. She cried somewhat silently, like it needed something more to make a sound. I hurt another girl in the passenger seat of my car. I knew it would happen in this car. Maybe it was a curse, your curse, Dad. The punishment for using a dead father's car. I wondered then if this was your way of communicating with me, expressing your shame at my failure as a son for abandoning my mother.

The snow fell faster, swallowing the car as we drove to her apartment. When we arrived, my gas light turned on, so I shut the car off to conserve the rest of the fuel. We lingered there for awhile. I didn't mind. If nothing else, I owed her silence.

"It's her, isn't it," she said.

"Yes. And no. It's complicated."

"I knew this would happen. Why do I keep trying?" She laughed through a cry. She didn't sound angry or hurt. She sounded matter-of-fact.

"Keep trying?" I said.

Her red eyes searched my face for irony. "Yes, Eddie. Keep trying. Did you think you're my first boyfriend?"

I didn't. Or at least, not consciously. Not logically. That was the problem. In my gut, I was a kid, and I just expected to be her first, as I was for Elizabeth. I was a fool. And now, I not only had nothing, I realized I had never had anything.

Snowflakes continued to fall from blackness. It was so quiet in the car, I could hear the flakes' barely audible taps into the windshield and their final cracklings as they dissolved.

Lisa leaned over, kissed me on the cheek, and left my car. I watched her open her apartment door, enter the darkness, and shut the door behind her without looking back. I sat in my car in front of her apartment for another fifteen minutes. A homeless man covered in snow rummaged through the dumpster across the lot. After he left, a teenage couple felt safe enough to exit their car, holding hands. I wanted to warn them.

26.

I stood in the bathroom staring in the vanity mirror at tiny red cracks in the whites of my eyes. They pulsated in my sunken face. I had lost my appetite since my last night with Lisa. At least when I was with her, I was with a kind human being who looked like Elizabeth. Now I had nothing and no one. Except Mom.

I shut off the bathroom lights and headed to bed. I peeked into Mom's room to say goodnight. She was already under the covers. Her nightstand light was on. The curtains on the French doors leading to the veranda were pulled back. The moon illuminated the neighbor's woodpile.

"What took you so long?" she said.

"My eyes are bloodshot. I—had to brush my teeth."

"What?" She was half asleep.

"Nothing. Had to brush my teeth. Wanted to say goodnight before I went in."

"Why did it take you so long?"

"It didn't."

"I'm not feeling well, Eddie." She turned. Her face was pale. There were dark circles under her eyes. She had changed so much since I was a child. Her lame smile had lowered. Pronounced wrinkles cluttered her forehead and the corners of her eyes and mouth. When had she aged so?

"Do you need anything?" I said.

"Come sit next to me."

I sat next to her on the bed. "Do you still think about Dad?" I asked.

"Every night."

"What was he like?"

"He wasn't perfect," she said, her eyes weighted. "We argued—he worked too much. You've been there for me."

"But he loved us, right?"

"Sure did love. Lo—" she said, nodding into dream.

I saw a prescription bottle in a half opened drawer of her nightstand. I leaned over to take a closer look: *Prescriber: Bleakman, Brian.*

"He loved—me. Loves me—love me—" She fell asleep.

I sat next to her on the bed and watched the clock on the wall. I thought back to that last day you were alive, when Mom wouldn't kiss you. Did she regret not having that last moment back like I did with Elizabeth? My memory of her was so vivid, so real I could have tasted her, I could have smelled her, sitting right there in Mom's room.

And then I did.

It was a scent of something sweet, a smell like the distant echo of windchimes. At first, it was too quick for my nose. The room was quiet. All was in its usual place. The scent settled. The bed rocked from my sudden movement. Mom stirred.

"Eddie, could you get me some water?" she said in a groggy voice.

"Sure." I hopped off the bed and walked down the hallway past pictures of Mom, Grandma, and me. None of you since the day of the burning.

The scent grew stronger as I entered the kitchen. It stopped me in the doorway. The kitchen lights illuminated the cherry stained wood cabinets around the perimeter. The kitchen lamp was on in front of the bay window overlooking the backyard. Mom used some of the money from your death to update the kitchen. No matter how many alterations or renovations were made, it never did feel quite like home.

My bare feet on the cold tiles made me shiver. I searched through the neat counters, inside some of the cabinets, and even the dishwasher. The scent was so strong, and yet I couldn't name or find it. The sky was a midnight blue, and against its royal darkness, a yellow box on the kitchen table caught my eye. It was a small container of tea that read *Jasmine* on the outside. I leaned over, opened the box, and inhaled.

Grandpa, your father, died a few years ago. We didn't even attend the wake. I saw him fewer and fewer times after you died. From what I remember, he didn't get along with Mom or Mom's mom. I remember Mom yelling at him on the phone a few times, but when she knew I was listening, she'd go into the other room to talk. During one of his visits many years ago, he had sat right where I was sitting. He sipped his tea slowly. Always the same tea. He loved it so much he would bring his own tea bags around with him.

"Grandpa, why do you always drink that tea?"

He looked at me, then back out the window. He was a quiet man with jawline that looked like carved stone. When he spoke, everyone listened. His gray eyes made you uncomfortable, as if they could penetrate skin, see all your sins and secrets, maybe see things you didn't know were there. He spent most of his time in that chair, drinking that tea and staring out the window. When I'd ask him if he wanted to do something, he would say, "I'm content." I didn't know much of his past, just that your mom died soon after she gave birth to you. Then you died, his only son. I guess after losing the two most important people in his life, he held onto anything he could.

"I always see you drinking that same tea. Don't you ever get tired of it? Don't you ever want to try something else? Mom has a whole cabinet of different teas."

He stopped mid-sip and put down his mug. He looked over at me with those eyes of his. "Sit down."

I sat.

"If I like something—" He paused. He closed his eyes and inhaled as if he might never smell it again. "If I choose to love something, like tea, I stick with it. I make a commitment. Your mom is a lover of many teas. I like one tea."

"I didn't mean to—"

"I just want you to know that." We sat there for a couple minutes longer in silence while he sipped his tea and stared out the window. "I was young when I met your grandma. I'm sorry you never met her. She would have been a great role model for you."

"What was she like?"

"She wore a scent." He called perfume a scent. "This tea," he said reaching into his pocket and pulling out a white pouch of black leaves, "is the same scent your grandmother used to wear."

"You bought the tea because it smells like Grandma?"

"I was in the grocery store when I smelled it, two aisles over. It led me right to its aisle and up to its square little box. The tea found me."

"How's that possible?"

"It found me."

I didn't believe him then. And yet, there I was, sitting at the very table where he told me his story, staring at a small box of tea that I smelled from Mom's bedroom, that smelled like Elizabeth.

I picked up the box of tea and inhaled again. Uncanny how similar it was to her. It hadn't even occurred to me that Elizabeth had a scent, but I supposed we all do. I pulled out the tea kettle and filled it with water. After turning the stove on, I set it down on the red dot. My feet were numb. I needed socks. The house was quiet as I moved through it. I walked to the entrance of Mom's room. She was no longer in bed. Light leaked out from under her closed bathroom door. I pressed my ear to the warm door and heard the shower running.

"Mom, you okay?" No response. "Mom?" I knocked a little louder. The shower shut off. I waited, then tried to turn the knob with little hope from a childhood filled with turning locked door knobs. I held my breath, praying she wasn't naked, and for some reason, imagining scenes of blood and sharp objects. When I opened the door and peered into the room, there, standing with a white towel around her bronze body, was Elizabeth, staring back at me in the mirror. She turned to face me, and I stumbled and fell to the ground and onto my back.

She walked out of the bathroom in a cloud of steam that encircled her tan skin and the bleach white towel. She was a windblown dandelion. Her wet hair fell to just above her chest. She stood with her left knee partially bent in toward her right thigh, her right arm on the frame of the bathroom door. Her outline glowed in the bathroom light. She hadn't changed since high school.

"What's wrong?" she said.

"Nothing. I mean—nothing. But how are you there?"

"Don't you want me to be?" she said.

"I'm sorry I let you go. I'm sorry about Lisa. Everything."

"It's okay. But we have to stop meeting like this."

"I don't mind," I said from the floor.

"Can I lie next to you in bed?" I asked.

"Let's—"

The tea kettle whistled from the kitchen.

"I put some tea on."

"It reminded you of me," she said.

"Most things do," I said. "I have to get the tea."

"Don't waste time."

"You know me," I said. We both smiled. Her cheeks flushed and her nose scrunched. There we were again, her glowing, standing above me, staring down at me on the ground, on my back like something fallen from the sky.

I picked myself up and ran out of the room and into the kitchen. The kettle screamed until I poured the steaming water into two mugs. I picked up two Elizabeth-scented-tea-bags and dropped one in each mug. I dumped a couple teaspoons of sugar in both and put a cube of ice in each so they wouldn't be too hot to drink. The cubes crackled as I walked the steamy, Elizabeth-scented-water back into the bedroom. The bathroom door was open, and the light was still on, but there was a lump under Mom's blanket. I shuffled over to it and set the mugs down on the nightstand next to her body.

"Tired already? I haven't—" I pulled back the covers.

"What are you doing?" Mom said. Her eyes were half shut.

Everything is real when you don't expect them to be.

"It's tea," I said. "I thought—" I began, but a ringing started in my ears and swelled and filled my head until I placed my hands around my skull as I watched Mom's mouth move without voice. She was talking. She was saying something to me, but all I heard was a ringing like Mr. Nostaga's tuning fork back in high school after he'd slam it against a music stand and hold it up to a silent band, and we'd all just watch and listen and never forget the pitch. It slowly faded to a dull lull, like the hum of fluorescent lights, and Mom's voice gradually returned.

"—nted was water," Mom finished, looking at the mugs. "Forget it." Then she pulled the covers back over her head.

The steam rose from the hot water but disintegrated immediately. The scent stayed. It lingered in the air, in my head. I sipped the tea and swallowed the scent.

"Turn that bathroom light off," Mom said from under the covers.

The bathroom door remained open, the light bleeding out onto a section of carpet. I could still see her glowing outline. Her figure in front of the open door—an open door. I shut the light off, went to bed, and dreamed of lying in an open doorway during a rainstorm.

27.

Shhh. . . Do you hear it? Snow hitting the ground? It makes a sound like God hushing the world. Is it snow, or dust from the ceiling, falling onto the carpet, or air leaving my lungs?

Something hits the window pane next to me. I move the blinds and open the window. Cool air rushes inside the stale, empty apartment for the first time.

A small bluebird is on its back, twitching on the sill. Bent wings. Crooked yellow toothpicks for legs. In its final twitchy moments, it must break its heart it can't speak what I can't see. I know it breaks mine.

Mom is probably still crying. When I left, her face was red and her hands were shaking while gripping the frame of the front door, waving, blowing kisses. Mumbling things like "Don't leave," and "You're all I have." I couldn't look at her while driving away. I'm only a town away from Mom, but with every mile that I drove, the heaviness in my chest grew as if someone were adding weights on top of my ribcage.

There's a knocking in my apartment. I wait, expecting it to go away. There's another. And another. Someone's at my door.

I get up, dizzy, and move slowly to the door.

"Who is it?"

"Eddie? It's Mom."

I look behind me—a room with a few chairs, unpacked boxes, and empty medication bottles on a fold-up table next to the window. What'll she think? I crack the door. She's wearing makeup, maybe too much.

From what I can remember, she hasn't worn makeup since you were alive. Except maybe when she went to Bleakman's office with me. The apartment complex hallway is dark. She's wearing short sleeves, no coat, and shorts.

"Aren't you cold?" I ask.

"Cold? No. Why?"

Snow. I can only think of snow and winter.

"Are you okay, Eddie? I haven't heard from you in three days."

Three days. It feels much longer. She moves closer to the door and tries to peek inside.

I close the door a little to block her view. "I'm fine. I have company. Why didn't you call?"

"I did," she says. She pulls out her cell phone. "I tried about ten times over the last few days. That's why I came by. It went right to voicemail."

"It's dead." My stomach cramps, and I wince.

"Who's in there?"

"Just a friend from high school."

She can tell I'm lying. I know she can tell because she knows that all my friends died with you in high school.

"Are you taking your—"

"Yes, Mom. Yes. I have to go."

"Call me if you need anything."

"I'll call you," I say, but I know I won't. I close the door, run to the bathroom, and dry heave. Nothing comes out. My colorful medications are still dissolving at the bottom of the toilet bowl in brown water. I flush it and watch the medications spiral up then sink into the black hole.

28.

The trees were bending to me, for me. I was on the swing in the backyard, expecting to puke. Mom was gardening, pulling weeds and pruning shrubs. It was snowing and sunny. Elizabeth's lawn gnome was there. "You're an idiot, Eddie." I'm an idiot. I *am* an idiot. "Eddie, come to church with me," Mom said in her polka dotted sundress. She moved a piece of hair off her forehead. A chunk of hair fell to the ground and turned to snow. "You see what happens when you don't spend time with me? I fall to pieces," she said. "Who does snow remind you of? Don't speak. Just think." *Elizabeth.* She threw her shovel down and it turned to snow. I heard a buzzing like electricity. "Come with me to church. You could use a little God in your life." *I could use a little God in my life. I could use a lot of God in my life. I could use some snow.*

Then we were in church, sitting in a pew. Three sections. We were in the middle section on the end of the pew in the front row. People were too close. Too many people, barely enough room to sit. When was the last time I was in church? *God forgive me.* I can remember being in church with you and Mom. An organ played, I watched your mouth as you sang, a warm voice. It made me warm, if I can remember what warmth feels like. You hadn't shaved. That I remember. And, yes, you weren't wearing a white t-shirt and jeans. You wore a collared shirt, button down, black pants. Your shoes were shiny. And you looked at me and said—

"Have mercy on us. Lamb of God," the cantor said. Mom repeated the phrase. I was drooling, I wiped my mouth with my sleeve. "Don't do that, Eddie. Use a tissue." She grabbed a tissue from her purple purse and wiped my mouth. "I got it, I got it. I'm not a child," I said.

The tall, black priest stood in front of the large congregation to recite the homily. He looked familiar. I had seen him before, high in the air, on top of the burning church. When he closed his eyes and mouth, he had no face at all. A giant Jesus on the cross hung behind him. *It must be nice to have Christ behind you.* "Eddie, don't speak that way," Mom said. Did I say it aloud? "Christ is behind you," Mom said. I looked behind me, but I didn't see Christ, I saw Lisa and her father, two pews back. He looked just like she did. She was smiling again. I turned my head before she saw me.

The priest began his speech. He had a strange accent and talked about something grave, but I don't remember what, then he stopped. He looked at me from the altar. "Mom? Why is he looking at me?" Mom was frozen, you too, looking up at the altar. Everyone in the church was quiet, crystallized. No one moved, the world had paused. It began to snow. I just remember snow, large flakes. I took out my pocket-watch, but the hands were missing. I read the inscription again, *Now is the time.* That's not right. *It's about time.* That's not right either.

The priest walked to me until he was in front of my pew. "Eddie, it's almost that time," he said.

"I need my father," I said. But you were gone, Dad. A pile of snow remained where you had once sat. Instead of ashes, I got snow.

"Is this another side effect of coming off the medication?" I said to the priest.

"It's a side effect of burying the dead." He elevated his hand as if he wanted me to stand.

I stood.

"In the name of the father, and of the son, and of the holy spirit," he said, giving me the sign of the cross, touching my forehead with his thumb. Always the thumb. "Did you hear that, Eddie? The father and the son. You can't separate them, no matter how many pills you take."

It was still snowing. The priest's shoulders were covered in white powder, but I was warm.

"Am I supposed to feel differently?" I asked.

"You tell me."

"What now?"

"Now, the benediction."

He wound his fist back and punched me clean through the center of my chest. It sounded like watermelons smashing. I couldn't breathe. The lights went out. All that remained was the ting of a tuning fork.

29.

Somewhere, in the blinding white, I see Elizabeth holding the gold pocket-watch up in the sun. It dangles from her hand, its yellow reflection marking my chest. "Even snowflakes fall in love with the ground before the end," she says. She lies on the bed, motioning for me to come to her in the light of a window.

Breath leaves - Hairs stand - Goose bumps rise

I am air

I am light

I open my eyes to see

and see—

30.

—an open window. I'm on my apartment floor freezing. I run to the bathroom and kneel on the cold tile before the toilet bowl, but I can't throw up. The urge is strong, but it won't come out of my body. My chest is sore. I raise my shirt and find a fist-sized purple bruise in the center. I stick my pointer down my throat, hitting the reflex, and heave, but nothing comes. I try again, deeper this time, scratching the back of my throat. I gag, feel the burn rise halfway. I miss Mom.

I try one more time. I use two fingers, my pointer and middle, and shove them as far back as possible until they hit something hard in the back of my throat, tapping something more solid than flesh. Up and out it comes, a gurgle of splattering and splashing into the clear water of the bowl. Once I start vomiting, I can't stop. More and more. Mostly yellow, stringy bile, and some solid balls that resemble nothing I remember swallowing. It burns and I can't breathe—it comes out of my nose, stings the inside of my skull. The more I vomit, the darker the vomit becomes. Then blood. Light pink, a clear red, then the color of red wine. The vomit shades blacken, thick and lumpy. I'm losing breath. With each heave, spasm, jerk of my body, more and more dark liquid and chunks pour forth. After the last spurt, I fall back against the wall next to all my things still in boxes and I gasp, a deep inhale. Darkness swells around my eyes.

When the room brightens, a shadow hovers over the toilet bowl. My mouth is acrid. I sit up, wipe my eyes of tears, and lean forward. An arm wavers from the black, foul stench of the bowl. Then an elbow. The hand grabs the rim of the porcelain and pulls a mass of vomit up from the muck. I kick my legs away, twisting my body around, and scurry on all fours into the bedroom like a squirrel dodging traffic. Where have you gone, Dad? Where is *my* hero of yesterday, the hero who never was but should have been? I listen with my body pressed against the wall.

Drops of water splatter on the tile, wet steps, slow. I close my eyes. I'll take the medicine.

More steps – slosh – slosh – across the bathroom tiles, a gurgle like the plunging of a clogged toilet, then silence. I wait and listen to my chest throb.

"Eddie."

I keep my eyes shut.

"Eddie."

Elizabeth. Elizabeth. Eliz—

"Open your eyes, Eddie."

I open my eyes and see, and see—me. It's me talking to me. Me looking at me. Me covered in my own vomit, naked, insecure, undeniably me, wiping the remaining vomit off of his body with a towel from the bathroom.

"Fuck you," I say.

"It's nice to see you too," he says. "Can I sit down?" He points to a spot on the floor in front of me.

"If I say no, are you going to crawl back into the vomit you came from?"

"Try not to end on a preposition."

"What do you want?"

"You don't seem surprised I'm here." He sits down. "You had a feeling it would come to this," he says.

"Can you put the towel on your—you know," I turn my head and point to his crotch. He's sitting cross-legged.

"It's not like I'm a complete stranger," he laughs.

I focus on his face, gaunt and pale, like a Munch painting. His eyes are the color of wet clay in the darkness of the room.

"You look like shit. Try eating something."

"Try losing your father."

"I have," he laughs again.

He's funny, but I know I can't tell him that he's funny. "Wish I could laugh at that."

"You should try laughing. You're so damn serious all the time. You still think you can do this? You're not even close. That's some heavy shit they've had us on."

"What happened to ending on a preposition?"

"Touché."

I'd punch myself in the face if I knew it would hurt him. "I can do this," I say through my chattering teeth.

"Are you going to cry?"

"No."

"You sound like you're going to cry."

"I'm not."

"It's always about you. Can't even take care of your mom—his dying wish." His face pinches. "And don't get me started on Elizabeth. She's probably fucking someone else right now because you couldn't get it up."

Before I know what I'm doing, I leap at him and land a punch across his jaw. The impact sends him back a few feet onto the carpet, but he rises and tackles me to the ground. He traps me in a headlock, both of us still on all fours, and slams me in the face, punch after punch. With each punch, a flash of memory—your orange-lit face—a moth caught in a spider's web—shadows ablaze. The images explode across my eyes as I feel the skin split on my forehead. I grab his left ankle and pull it hard out and across the floor. We both spill into the bathroom now. His body twists and he falls to his side. I stand and land kick after kick into his ribcage. He spits blood. I stomp on his ribs, on his lower back, but this isn't enough for me. I need more. I want blood. I need something deeper than blood. I mount him, each one of my knees on each one of his arms, pinning him, trapping him. His arms are outstretched as if preparing to be nailed in position. I assault his face and head with punches. And then I see me. I'm staring at my own cut face. I take his head in my hands, my head. I raise it high off the floor, and with all of the strength I have left, I slam it hard onto the tile, over, and over, and over. Darker, and darker, and darker the room grows as I scream, and slam, and crack my head against the floor until it gives, until it cracks open, bloodied and vulnerable—I collapse.

31.

The sun is shining. The window is open. The blinds are raised. Children are laughing somewhere. They sound like summer. Like something I want to be a part of. Like nothing I can remember.

It's quiet. I'm not dead. I'm not even close to death. I'm not bloody, or cut, or bruised. I felt this way once. It's not what I remember. It's better. The memory is never as good. Is this happiness? Not yet—but close.

I want to scream. Can I? A good scream. I'm actually smiling, not remembering smiling. I can feel my face smiling. It's warm. Everything is warm. I forgot how much I love warmth. I need to leave. This apartment is too small for what I need. So I go. But not before taking the picture of us on ice skates and slipping it into my pocket.

It's five o'clock. The sun has already begun to set. There are no other cars on the road. A family—a mom, dad, and daughter—stand on a sidewalk. They stare down the street as if waiting for a parade, a homecoming. Their eyes follow my car as I drive by. I open the windows. The air doesn't feel quite like air. It's thicker, like liquid soap. My car hasn't driven this way since I first drove it. Only a subtle rumbling every once in a while, but nothing like it was. When Elizabeth and I used to drive together. Mom's car is in the driveway as I pull up to the house. My stomach growls. How long has it been since I've eaten?

When I open the front door, the sun from behind me blankets the furniture, stairs, walls, and floor in gold. I close the door and darkness fills the space. I listen for the disheartening quiet. But it's gone. A tick here. A creak there. A dog bark. And where is Mom? I move into the kitchen and rummage through the fridge. Cheese, mayo, pumpernickel bread, some potato salad with a torn label. If the potato salad is expired, I won't throw up. I've met my lifetime-vomiting-quota. I cram it all on a sandwich and into my mouth, inhaling and exhaling heavily through my nose. When I finish, I walk into the living room and lie on the couch, pregnant with food. The room is as it has always been, no pictures of you. I watch the sun drench everything in orange as it sets. Particles float around the room as if underwater. I fall asleep: no ribcage, no snow, no Elizabeth, no mom, no you. I dream of nothing.

When I awake, the room is dark, and I am hanging halfway off the couch. I sit up, lean across the cocktail table, and turn on a lamp next to an old, leather-cover copy of the Bible. The page's edges are gold. Something sharp is digging into my thigh. I reach into my pocket and pull out the picture of you and me. It's bent on the corner now, so I use the Bible to iron out the crease. There's a loud creak from above. You once told me that this sound is the house settling. You forgot to tell me that a house never finishes settling. This house needs you. The walls are covered with decorative copy prints Mom bought at Target and a few pictures of Grandma, and Mom, and me. This isn't a home. Not yet.

Mom keeps your tools in the basement. I grab your hammer and a single nail—it's all I have. I walk back upstairs and take down the photograph of Grandma standing next to a chapel in a floral sundress—now is the time. With the photograph of us pressed and leveled to the bulging beam in the wall, the nail centered at the top of it, I raise the hammer and strike the nail over and over into the wall, deeper and deeper into the beam, until it is flush and holding the photo in place. This is where you belong.

"Eddie, you're home?" Mom says from the entrance of her room. She approaches and flicks the hall light on. She's squinting, arms crossed over her chest. Her oversized white robe drags behind her.

"I am home," I say, looking around the room.

"How's the apartment?"

"I'm not staying there anymore."

"So you're coming back home?"

"I'm not sure. I don't think so."

She looks at the hammer in my hand. "It's 2am. What were you doing?" Her hair is messy and thin. She steps closer.

I look up at the picture of us as if you would speak for me. But there's something different about the photo now that it's on the wall. It's you. Your face. It's not cut off. It's never been cut off. Your entire self is in the picture. Your brown hair, gray eyes, stubbled face. And your smile. How could I forget that smile?

"I—Dad. It's Dad, Mom."

She looks up at the picture on the wall. Her hand cups her mouth.

"What's wrong?" I put my hand on her bony shoulder.

"Why did you do that?" she says. "Where did you get that picture? I thought—"

"—you burned them all?"

She looks at me as if I had spoken to the dead.

"I followed you that day. Into the backyard. I watched you burn all the photos of him. Except this one. Did you think I wouldn't wonder why we didn't have any pictures of him around the house?"

"No—I mean, I knew you'd wonder. Having pictures of him wasn't as important as—"

"As what?"

"As you being—okay. Normal."

"Normal? Is this what you call normal?"

"It's what we thought was right."

"We?"

"Me and Grandma. We thought it would help you."

I cup my hands around her face and whisper, "Forgetting is not grieving."

"I tried my best," she says. "What about me? Who was—who's going to take care of me?"

"I did my best, Mom."

She leans in to kiss me, but I turn my cheek. I turn my cheek for you. I turn my cheek for her, for me. And I'll turn my cheek from this time forward. I hug her. We remain in the center of the room. I hold her for awhile, listening for the ceiling to creak. It doesn't.

"You look just like him. It's a good picture. I remember it."

"You were there?"

"Who do you think took the photo? We were all there. It was fun. We had a lot of fun together."

"I can't be Dad."

"I know," she says.

She looks up at the photo one last time. "I'll get a frame for it tomorrow." Then she walks to her bedroom door and looks back at me. "Why don't you get some sleep? We can get your stuff from the apartment tomorrow and move it—wherever you want to move it."

"I will in a few minutes. I just need some water," I say.

"Goodnight, Eddie. I love you."

"I love you too, Mom."

She pauses at her bedroom entrance, then she vanishes into the darkness of her room.

I don't go to bed. There's a spot on my chest that itches, and every time I scratch, it moves. Maybe the itch is under my skin.

32.

In the beginning was Elizabeth, and Elizabeth was in light, and Elizabeth was light. I stood outside her window and watched as it rained from a cracked ceiling.

And now, I am outside in the night once again, peering into her dark home from behind a bush with my car parked down the street. I pick up a pebble and toss it at her bedroom window. And another. Her bedroom light turns on. Eyes appear at the pane, then vanish. It begins to rain, softly at first. Then it pours. The hall light turns on then off, a trail of lights—on and off and on and off and on—as she moves through the house—she truly is light.

The rain is heavy now, bloated drops. Elizabeth's living room illuminates. The curtains are pulled back as usual. I hide my head behind the bush and watch through branches. She stands next to the television looking out the window. She's wearing a semi-transparent, white nightgown. She looks the same. Her face is tan in the light of the room. I can even see a few of her larger freckles, her larger earlobe. Elizabeth opens the window. The light from behind her is eclipsed, leaving only a silhouette of her body. Her arms rise as she leans against the frame and the wings of her nightgown fall, expand, and prepare for flight. Some of the light penetrates the material under her arms.

"Is it you?" she calls out into the night.

I want to answer her this time. I want to be her you. I want to be someone's you. I want to be your you, Dad.

The rain stops altogether. A section of the sky clears above, but the stars aren't visible, and the moon is new.

"It *is* you," she says.

I don't speak because I know I can be many things for Elizabeth. I can be many things for Mom, and Grandma, and even myself. I can even be something for you, Dad. But I know I can't be you. I watch Elizabeth wait for a reply. I hear her breathe. My ribs creak. The lawn gnome rests at the base of the steps, but he's just stone now. His colors have faded.

Elizabeth turns and shuts the living room light off.

"Wait," I yell. "It's—me." My eyes struggle to adjust to the darkness as I stumble toward her house, toward the window where she was, where she is. I know she's still there. I can feel it. I know she heard me, her hand on the light switch, straining to hear my straining to see.

No, I can't see. But I will. I keep my eyes open because I will see greater things than these. This much, I know.

Acknowledgements

I'm incredibly blessed with a loving and supportive wife, Ashleigh, our daughters, Evelyn and Dylan, and my patient and loyal family—Mom, Dad, Melissa, and Eddie.

A special thanks to the "Dream Team"—Stephanie Harper, Scott Schilling, Devon Bohm, and Allison Wagner—and to The Fairfield Scribes.

Thank you to my Fairfield MFA community and all my former mentors.

I am also grateful for the support and encouragement of my former Wilton High School colleagues and my current Great Neck North High School colleagues.

And to Friend Burton, who helped me to feel and not think.

Past Titles

Running Wild Stories Anthology, Volume 1

Running Wild Anthology of Novellas, Volume 1

Jersey Diner by Lisa Diane Kastner

Magic Forgotten by Jack Hillman

The Kidnapped by Dwight L. Wilson

Running Wild Stories Anthology, Volume 2

Running Wild Novella Anthology, Volume 2, Part 1

Running Wild Novella Anthology, Volume 2, Part 2

Running Wild Stories Anthology, Volume 3

Running Wild's Best of 2017, AWP Special Edition

Running Wild's Best of 2018

Build Your Music Career From Scratch, Second Edition by Andrae Alexander

Writers Resist: Anthology 2018 with featured editors Sara Marchant and Kit-Bacon Gressitt

Magic Forbidden by Jack Hillman

Frontal Matter: Glue Gone Wild by Suzanne Samples

Mickey: The Giveaway Boy by Robert M. Shafer

Dark Corners by Reuben "Tihi" Hayslett

The Resistors by Dwight L. Wilson

Upcoming Titles

Running Wild Stories Anthology, Volume 4
Running Wild Novella Anthology, Volume 4
Open My Eyes by T.E. Hahn
Legendary by Amelia Kibbie
Christine, Released by E. Burke
Recon: The Anthology by Ben White
The Self Made Girl's Guide by Aliza Dube
Sodom & Gomorrah on a Saturday Night by Christa Miller
Turing's Graveyard by Terry Hawkins
Running Wild Press, Best of 2019

Running Wild Press publishes stories that cross genres with great stories and writing. Our team consists of:

Lisa Diane Kastner, Founder and Executive Editor
Barbara Lockwood, Editor
Cecile Sarruf, Editor
Peter Wright, Editor
Piper Daniels, Editor
Benjamin White, Editor
Andrew DiPrinzio, Editor
Amrita Raman, Operations Manager
Lisa Montagne, Director of Education

Learn more about us and our stories at www.runningwildpress.com

Loved this story and want more? Follow us at
www.runningwildpress.com, www.facebook.com/runningwildpress, on
Twitter @lisadkastner @JadeBlackwater @RunWildBooks

CPSIA information can be obtained
at www.ICGtesting.com
Printed in the USA
FSHW021825211119
64368FS